The Unlikely World of Faraway Frankie

Keith Brooke (signature)

Keith Brooke

A Special signed Edition, Limited to
200 numbered copies.
This is number:

60

The Unlikely World of Faraway Frankie

Keith Brooke

With an introduction by
Adam Roberts

NewCon Press
England

First edition, published in the UK April 2010
by NewCon Press
41 Wheatsheaf Road, Alconbury Weston, Cambs, PE28 4LF

NCP 026 (signed hardback)
NCP 027 (signed softback)

10 9 8 7 6 5 4 3 2 1

ISBN:

978-1-907069-12-3 (hardback)
978-1-907069-13-0 (softback)

Cover illustration by Dean Harkness
Cover layout and design by Andy Bigwood

Book layout by Storm Constantine

Printed in Great Britain by the MPG Books Group, Bodmin and King's Lynn

For Debbie

The Unlikely World of Faraway Frankie: An introduction

Adam Roberts

Some writers write exclusively for adults; some exclusively for children; but the most enduring works of literature – from Robinson Crusoe to Le Guin's *Earthsea*, from *Pilgrim's Progress* to Tolkien, from *Alice in Wonderland* to *Harry Potter* – are loved by children and adults alike. This, I'd say, is the hardest writerly discipline of all to master: to write a book that surpasses the tendency to categorise literature into 'young adult' and 'old adult' categories. Keith Brooke's *The Unlikely World of Faraway Frankie* is a masterclass in how to transcend those sorts of labels. It is wiser about youth and imagination than most other novels published today; and everybody, of whatever age, should read it.

The Unlikely World of Faraway Frankie is not only a marvelously compelling exploration of a fantastical world, but a meditation upon the nature of fiction itself. The main character, Frankie Finnegan, is as blithe and honest as his first name suggests; and like the Finnegan from the nursery rhyme he demonstrates the ability, common amongst children but relatively rare in adults, to begin-again. Indeed, his doing so constitutes the main trajectory of this novel, and lends its lustre to the novel's powerful ending. Of course we root for him, and want him to succeed; and where this wonderful novel is so canny is in the way it shows precisely the degree to which *wanting* is a tangled and contradictory business.

Like most kids, Frankie is not the fittest, or thinnest, or most popular boy in school; and like many kids he has known more than his fair share of sorrow. The world is not the way he might like it to be: school is a drag, he is bullied, his family is broken. In some ways Frankie is a young Walter Mitty – like Mitty, he is a dreamer whose fantasies have greater purchase upon his mind than reality. But Brooke's fable takes us into a beyond-Mitty state where the dream not only dominates life but literally comes true, where Frankie discovers that a wish fulfilled is a much more complicated and dangerous thing than a wish unfulfilled. We know the cliché 'be careful what you wish for – you might get it'. As is the case with many clichés, over familiarity robs us of the sentiment's bladed sharpness. Brooke's novel makes it come dangerously alive in our minds. The translation of his old town into his 'Faraway' is only the start of a deeper, more compelling fictional narrative of self-discovery.

> He remembered what it had been like when all this had been fresh and new. He remembered *imagining* a creek stopping Barking and Stu from catching him. He remembered *imagining* the town with hunched up cobbled streets and gas lamps just like the Faraway he and Grace had always talked about. He remembered *imagining* that school would no longer intrude on their idyllic summer holiday lives.

The novel is about this power and hazards of imagination in a more profound sense than just wish-fulfilment. It is about having the power to create a world – the power authors take for granted. As such this is more than just a story about a boy. It is a story about Story. Its self-reflexive, or metafictional, element is neatly underplayed, but it is there: Frankie's friend Wookie has a real name; and it's the same as the name as the writer in whose tale the two appear (just as Wookie's surname hovers rhyme-like over the author's surname). Frankie takes all the stories he knows and parleys them into a new world; he is the author of his environment, and, by the novels end, of himself too.

This is not the first novel to do this, of course; but it is one of the most eloquent. One thing that makes it more effective than most is the way Brooke shows us that Frankie's power to imagine is contaminated by his grief, and guilt, at the death of his sister. His imaginative creation cannot help but be bent out of the shape by the gravitational force of death. His father (who, we are told, is unable to follow his true métier, funerals) works in the pier arcade surrounded by machines rather than living people and in Frankie's Faraway various living people are replaced by soulless automata. Frankie is continually being told not to interfere; to let things run on in their familiar, uncomfortable but reassuring grooves. Of course he *does* keep interfering. For one thing, he is driven to search for the mysterious individual with the symbolic name 'the Owner'. We might think this is the name given to the individual who 'owns' the fantasy world; but (of course) 'own' also means oneself – when you're on your own, there's just you. (Walter Mitty's surname likewise contains a self-reflexive 'me').

None of this would work half so well if Brooke didn't anchor it in a compellingly realised real world. His command of detail is superb:

> Mother had his dinner on a plate, under a damp tea-towel in the top oven on low to keep it warm and keep the moisture in. It was shepherd's pie, and he could taste the tea-towel on the potato.

It's not just the string of precisely observed, vividly recalled physical details; it's the way Brooke gets inside the details of his

9

cast. Frankie is bullied at school, but this is a novel that understands that when a kid is bullied the *last* thing she or he will do is burst into tears and run away. Frankie's laughter, his joking along with the kids who persecute him, the resilience of his desire to fit in, is beautifully, if a little heartbreakingly, observed. The precision of these moments (and there are a great many of them) prevents what is, otherwise, a wildly fluid fantasy world from flying off into the realms of the implausible. However weird things get, the book never feels alien.

So, this is a novel is about the imagination; about what we do in the face of the implacable unpleasantness of the world. It is about fantasy and fantasy's prophylactic quality. Just as Frankie spies on the world using a painted strongman façade as cover, so Fantasy itself interposes an augmented but flattened layer between us and the real world. Fantasy is sometimes criticized as 'escapist'; and there's a germ of truth in the accusation. But children understand better than adults that escape is *hard*: that its positive aura exists in uneasy relationship to its negative – not just (as with older adults) the sense of responsibility abdicated, but more alarmingly of abandonment and of *truancy*.

Early in 2009, psychologist Adam Phillips published an essay with the title 'In Praise of Difficult Children.'[1] And what is praiseworthy about difficult children?

> When you play truant you have a better time. But how do you know what a better time is, or how do you learn what a better time is? You become aware, in adolescence and in a new way, that there are many kinds of good time to be had, and that they are often in conflict with each other. When you betray yourself, when you let yourself down, you have misrecognised what your idea of a good time is; or, by implication, more fully realised what your idea of a good time

---

[1] *London Review of Books,* 12th Feb 2009

might really be. You thought that doing this – taking drugs, lying to your best friend – would give you the life you wanted; and then it doesn't. You have, in other words, discovered something essential about yourself; something you couldn't discover without having betrayed yourself. You have to be bad in order to discover what kind of good you want to be (or are able to be).

'You have discovered something essential about yourself; something you couldn't discover without having betrayed yourself.' Betrayal is a heavily loaded word, but this does articulate something about Frankie's own experience—except that Brooke takes this plangent insight one step further. Frankie plays truant not from school, but from reality. What he discovers about himself is precisely himself. It is (and I handle this Hollywood cliché with tongs, although it *is* appropriate here) the journey Frankie travels that makes this short novel one of the best things Brooke has ever written. He is able to convey, readably, entertainingly, that children have the capacity to apprehend the world with greater intensity, to live and play with more imaginative ferocity and joy. As Wordsworth wrote in his Intimations Ode, two centuries ago, growing-up is a process of losing this access to the sublime. The irony of the title is that *The Unlikely World of Faraway Frankie* turns out to be very likely indeed; it is our world, and reading Brooke's novel is simultaneously to travel to a far-out fantasy location, and to become reacquainted with the familiarities of our quotidian lives. Faraway is near at hand, and both are wonderfully evoked in this novel.

Adam Roberts, February 2010

The Unlikely World of Faraway Frankie

"Still, I had a clearer pleasure than this, which was the formation of castles in the air – the indulging of waking dreams – the following up trains of thought... my dreams were all my own; I accounted for them to nobody; they were my refuge when annoyed – my dearest pleasure when free."

Mary Shelley
Introduction to the Standard Novels
edition of *Frankenstein*, 1831

1. The Incident of The Mud On The Carpet

Frankie Finnegan slung his school bag over his shoulder and headed down Crestfallen Street towards the Drop. Across the road, three girls from Year Seven or Eight pointed and smirked. One of them said something but the only word Frankie could make out was "fatty".

He stopped and looked until he caught the eye of one of the girls, and then, with a grand flourish, he bowed low. The girls fell silent as he did this, then as he straightened one of them spoke and the three giggled and turned away from him.

Frankie grinned and started to walk again.

High up, a great big black and white gull yelled at him from a rooftop. The houses were squashed together here in neat lines along the hill-face, each with its own top-floor view out over the roofs of the houses below to the wide grey sea. Frankie only occasionally glimpsed the sea and the rooftops through gaps between the terraces of houses. The sky overhead was like an oil spill, great smudges of black and grey blocking out what sunlight there was this late in the year. The whole scene could have been a grainy black and white photograph.

Frankie loosened his tie.

At the end of Crestfallen Street was a corner shop with heavy metal grilles over the windows and graffiti on the walls. Frankie went inside. He took a Big Eat pack of salt and vinegar and a can of Coke and went up to the till. Cindy, with heavy mascara smeared around her eyes and standing-up black hair, stared at him, never interrupting the munch munch munch of chewing her gum. Cindy was an automaton, Frankie knew. The Owner put a great key in her back and wound her up at the start of every day, then he left her to work through her limited repertoire of behaviours. This was cheaper, and more reliable, than real staff.

"Hi, Frankie," she said, holding a thin hand up for his money. Black bangles throttled her wrist. "Good day at school?" Showing interest: a programmed response. She didn't mean it.

He handed her the right change. "Sure," he said. "I've been awarded a scholarship to study at the Illustrious Academy of Industrious Philatelists. They say I have a big future in the field of postal pricing studies. I'm not so sure, myself."

She nodded and said, "Sure, Frankie." She returned her attention to her magazine. Apparently, a wealthy footballer had had his house redecorated.

Frankie left the shop. He pulled open his bag of crisps as he came to the top of the flight of steps they called the Drop.

Ahead, he saw Barking and Stu, slowly riding their bikes down the steps at a precarious angle. It looked pretty cool, but Frankie knew he could do that just as well. If he had a bike, and if he had the strength and control, that is. Easy.

He flipped the can's ringpull open one-handed. Now *there* was a trick.

He paused on the steps halfway down, just past where the Drop crossed Rigormortis Road. Though the November afternoon was chilly, Frankie was aware of the sweat sticking his shirt to his back from the exertion. The exercise was good for him. People had told him that often enough.

From here, he could see out across Nereby-on-Sea to the wide sweep of the bay. Two white-sailed yachts were out there, cutting close to the end of the pier, where the lifeboat station bulged like the unwanted orange in the toe of a Christmas stocking. The sea was the colour of slate, the pier a line of charcoal and dirty white.

Frankie finished his crisps and washed them down with the last of his Coke before depositing the can and empty packet in a wire bin. He considered heading on down to the pier, where his father would be minding the one-armed bandits and dodgems, but no. Not today.

Not on the Birthday.

He turned left on Smugglers' Row instead, walking in the middle of the tarmac road because cars were parked up across the pavement. Soon, the street made a sharp turn to the right, and he saw The Jolly Old Sea Captain. The pub sign with its leering old bearded seaman had been the same for years, which was a shame, as it had given him nightmares as a small boy and sometimes still did. The Jolly Old Sea Captain, creaking in the breeze just outside his bedroom window.

Frankie came to the front door of the house next to the pub and took the key from his blazer pocket. He slid it into the lock, twisted, and pushed the door open.

Inside, he closed the door gently and stooped to remove his shoes and place them in the basket below the mirror. He stood, and looked at himself. With some spit on his hands he smoothed his hair down, knowing that it would be standing up at odd angles again in seconds. He put his bag into the cupboard beneath the stairs and went through to the kitchen.

Mother was there.

She sat at the table, cradling a cup of weak milky tea. He saw two empties on the table. Mrs Wotsit and Miss Thingy had been here then, doing the weekly grocery drop. A pot bubbled on the hob. Eye of newt for tea again. With pasta twists, by the look of it.

Mother.

A small woman, the top of her head only reached Frankie's chin, and she was so slight that if she stood sideways she would barely cast a shadow. She was wearing a black cardigan she had knitted herself, over a silky black blouse, with black lace gloves over the hands that clutched the cup.

She looked up at Frankie and placed her cup on the table.

"There is," she said, in a voice that somehow managed to sound both ominous and frail, "mud on the carpet." She paused for so long that Frankie thought she had finished, then added, "In the front room."

Frankie looked down immediately at his stockinged feet. "I..." he said, then stopped because he didn't have the faintest idea which words should follow. Then it came to him. "I'll clean up," he said.

Mother stood, and turned to inspect her cauldron of eye of newt and bats' eyebrows on the hob. Frankie reached up to a wall cupboard where he found an open packet of chocolate Hobnobs. He was careful to eat them over a plate to catch the crumbs.

"So tell me, Frankie," said Mother, stirring some strange powder into the brew, "how was your day?"

"It was a highly successful day, thank you, Mother. Headmaster Grimes only gave me five lashes of the cane, and I believe that I have learned my lesson and I will never again get my six and a quarter times tables wrong. I studied Chinese astrology and the art of tea-leaf divination in the morning, and sandstorm physics in the afternoon. And at lunchtime we were entertained handsomely by a troupe of wandering..."

Mother was watching him. "Really, you UGL," she said. This was a term of affection: Useless Great Lump. That was far better than the things she called Frankie's father whenever he dared show his face. "You and your daydreaming. You'll never get anywhere by daydreaming."

Except away, Frankie thought, as he licked a finger and used it to collect biscuit crumbs from his plate. Daydreams are all your own work: no one else to interfere, no one else to spoil things. In your daydreams you could write your own rules.

Mother was watching him, disapproving. "I sometimes wonder," she said, "whether you spend more time dreaming than you do in the real world."

He smiled and said nothing. Let her wonder what he was thinking.

The crumbs were all gone, so he stood and went to the cupboard under the sink for the dustpan and brush.

The door was of a heavy, dark wood, polished to an immaculate shine. Frankie took the handle, twisted and pushed. The room was gloomy, so stuffy you could almost see the air itself where shafts of daylight angled in through the heavy curtains. Frankie turned the light on and went in.

The sofa and armchair were very upright, with intricate flowery patterns and neatly arranged antimacassars of white linen with lace edging. The fireplace was made up with an orderly stack of coals and a layer of dust which showed how long it was since flames had last appeared here.

An oak sideboard stood against the innermost wall, and on it were dozens of photographs of Frankie's sister, Grace Elizabeth Finnegan. Grace as a babe in arms. Grace toddling with a heavy nappy bagged down to her dimpled little knees. Grace and Frankie with arms across each other's shoulders, about eight years old: two slim, handsome children with big doe-like eyes and the same dark hair. Grace on their eleventh birthday, all done up in her best, hints of an adult face beginning to emerge from beneath the puppy fat.

Amongst the photographs was an assortment of trinkets and souvenirs: a jagged conch shell, in which Grace had liked to listen to the sound of the sea; a small clay figure labelled "Grace", which Frankie had made years ago; a white ribbon, tied in a neat bow around nothing; a silver bracelet. And a vase, tall and slim, with a single flower in it: a large lily, its stark white trumpet speckled deep within its throat with black.

Frankie remembered why he had come in here. He looked down at the carpet. Just as Mother had said, a smudge of mud marred its pattern of grey and black squares. Two smudges.

He looked more closely. They were footprints, the mark of two feet, facing the sideboard.

He put a foot forward for comparison. The feet were smaller than his, and narrower.

Sherlock Holmes would have been able to read more into the prints, he thought. The great detective would probably have been able to say that the person responsible for the prints had a limp, and he would probably be able to make a pretty good guess at what they'd had for breakfast that morning.

Frankie kneeled to brush the dirt away.

The feet had been bare, too. He could see the imprint of the toes.

The stiff bristles of the brush blurred the prints, and soon they were gone, swept up into the plastic maw of the dustpan.

Frankie settled back on his heels and looked around the room. Nothing had been disturbed. There was no more mud, no more footprints.

Must have been Mother, he thought. She had finally cracked. She and her two friends had probably spent the day dancing naked in the garden in some Wicca ritual, and then trailed mud into the house. That would give the neighbours something to complain about.

He heard the rattle as someone pushed the front door, then three loud cracks of the iron door knocker. Frankie smiled. Father was home.

Frankie stood and backed out of the front room, closing the heavy door gently behind him. He opened the front door and smiled broadly. He had been right: it was his father. The small man stood with one foot on the doorstep. Thin strands of hair were combed across his shiny crown, while thick sideburns like iron wool crept down either jaw. "Son," he said. When he spoke, crooked grey teeth showed. His eyes jumped from place to place, never quite meeting Frankie's look.

"Father." Frankie stepped aside and his father entered the house. "How is the one-armed bandit today?"

Father hesitated, then grinned, and finally met Frankie's look. "He's fine," he said. "Sends his regards, Frankie. Sends his regards."

Frankie smiled.

"It's quarter past," said Mother, as the two of them entered the kitchen. Frankie couldn't tell whether she was informing Father he was late or early.

"My sweet," said Father in reply.

Frankie stepped out of the back door to empty the dustpan. Father had finally moved out of the family home two years ago, but he remained a regular visitor. "Your good mother," he had told Frankie shortly before he left, in one of the longest talks the two had had. "Can't live with her, can't live without her." Then he'd winked and added, "But I'm going to have a crack at the latter, I am."

Back in the kitchen, Frankie joined his parents at the table. They each had a cup of tea now, so Frankie reached across to get another can of Coke from the fridge.

"Fifteen today," said Father, eyes jumping from Frankie to Mother and around the kitchen. "She'd be –"

"None of that you useless clod," Mother snapped. "We're celebrating the Grace we knew, not what she might have been."

Frankie slurped at his drink and was repaid with a fierce look from Mother.

"Made a cake, have you?" asked Father brightly.

She nodded.

Frankie went to the fridge and removed the cake while Mother took candles from a drawer. The cake had been drizzled with dark chocolate icing, which had cascaded down the sides and set, so that the whole thing looked as if it had been caught just as it was starting to melt. It looked like something geological.

Mother counted out fifteen black candles in holders and then stabbed them into the cake.

She lit them from an extra-long kitchen match, and began to sing. "Happy birthday to you..."

Frankie sat quietly until they reached "...to Gra-ace" and then he stood, pushing his chair over with the back of his legs.

He left the room.

He took the stairs two at a time, then turned along the landing to the front bedroom. Inside, he leaned back against the door. His room was a mess, but he liked it that way. Or at least, he liked it better than having to tidy up. Clothes lay in heaps, and bulged out of drawers; magazines and sketch pads lay scattered about; little figures made from modelling clay stood along shelves and on the top of the chest of drawers; books stood in uneven stacks, just ready to fall.

He went to his bed and lay down, head cupped in his hands on the pillow. He thought back to the times when he and Grace had been inseparable. Long summer days, searching rock pools and playing hide and seek among the footings of the pier at low tide.

What would she look like now, if she was still alive? Would

she have put on the kilos like Frankie, or would she still be small like their parents? Small, he was sure. She'd still have her hair long so that it could be tied back with a ribbon when she wanted, and she'd still run twice as fast as he ever could.

He closed his eyes and saw her dashing across the sand and rocks. The colours were bright, almost *too* bright. The blue of the sky, the yellow of the sand. He could taste the salty breeze on his lips.

There was a knock at the door, and Frankie hastily rubbed at his eyes.

"Hmm?" he said.

The door opened a short way and his father poked his head round. Then he reached in and tossed a big rectangular object onto the bed. A bar of white chocolate.

He winked.

"Happy birthday, son," he said, and then was gone.

2. There Was A Young Boy

Frankie sat at his window and ate the bar of chocolate two squares at a time. Outside, the ever-present breeze swung the sign of The Jolly Old Sea Captain. For a time, Frankie allowed his vision to blur and he saw a cobbled street, a thick pea-souper fog swirling between the tightly-packed houses, a carriage pulled by a team of horses, rattling past. He had read too much Sherlock Holmes and Edgar Allan Poe.

He blinked, and it was dusk, cars parked up across the pavement, litter blowing in the breeze, the old sea captain swinging.

He thought of the things he had told Cindy and Mother about his day: the philately scholarship, being caned by Mr Grimes, the lessons in Chinese astrology and sandstorm physics. None of that was true, of course. He knew that. It was all in his head. All where he escaped to.

What really happened today was this.

It all started with the register, and went downhill from there.

They sat in their neat rows of desks, school bags at their feet. In silence. Mr Cray always insisted on silence.

"Stuart Daly?"

"Here, sir."

"Daisy Evans?"

"Here, Mr Cray."

"Frankie Finnegan?"

"Oh no he isn't," hissed more than one voice.

"Present, Mr Cray, sir," said Frankie, ignoring the tired old joke. *Frankie's fatagain – he'll never be finnegan.*

Mr Cray paused, and glowered at Frankie as if the disturbance had been his fault. Harry Barker poked Frankie in the backside with a ruler wedged under the laces of his shoe, and that might even have been when the damage was done, although Frankie would never be sure.

"Sir?" said Frankie, but Mr Cray returned to the register.

"Isaac Harvey?"

Afterwards, Mr Cray led them through to the hall for Upper School assembly. Instead of filing into the ranked seats, they went up on stage: this was 10CR's day in the spotlight, *their* assembly. For most, it was a once-a-year ordeal, but Frankie didn't mind. This was a chance to do something different, a chance to perform and not just be doing the mundane normal things.

Their theme, handed to them from on high, was Bullying Is Bad And Shall Be Punished In Hell. That wasn't quite how Mr Cray had put it. "Okay," he'd told his class, two weeks earlier. "We're going to do bullying in assembly."

"Isn't that bad, sir?" Frankie had asked, innocently. "Even in assembly?"

Mr Cray had let his comment go for once. "I thought we could act out a scenario and then let the protagonists explain their actions. You need to think things through, okay? Think about the motivations and the feelings of everyone involved. So who wants to be a bully?"

A forest of hands reached for the ceiling.

Mr Cray cleared his throat. "I see we'll need to audition... Okay. We need some targets for the bullies, too. Volunteers?"

No one.

Frankie looked around, and then, slowly, raised a hand. "Mr Cray, sir," he said. "I suppose... well, I suppose I could be the fat kid. At a pinch," he added hastily. "With some padding. But I'd be willing to give it my best shot, Mr Cray, sir."

After a brief pause, laughter had erupted around the room and Mr Cray had had another struggle on his hands to wrest control from a bunch of unruly fourteen- and fifteen year-olds.

Frankie had not needed to audition. He had been the only volunteer. And so today, he had played the victim in assembly in front of 500 other kids.

He had walked onto the stage, alone, and stood apart from the others, exactly as Mr Cray had told him. He let them call him names and jeer. They hadn't meant anything, of course. It was all play-acting. He wondered how many people really got how easy it was for his classmates to call names and be part of the crowd, and how hard it was to be on the other side of the name-calling even when they were only play-acting. Despite Mr Cray's attempts to direct, Frankie doubted that even he really understood.

"Hey, fatty!" Harry Barker drawled. "Lick my shoes, fatty."

Frankie got down on his knees, his back to the audience. He paused, glanced back over his shoulder, and then leaned forward as if he was trying to pray in the direction of Mecca.

A loud ripping sound echoed around the assembly hall. For an instant, Frankie thought the sound was someone breaking wind and then he realised what had happened. A sudden breeze somewhere unexpected informed him that his trousers had split at the seam exposing his slinky white boxer shorts to the world.

He consoled himself with the thought that they were clean, at least, and had no inappropriate holes. They even had a rather fetching ribbed pattern on the stretch fabric. Those in the front row would have an excellent view of the pattern, although it might be harder to make out from the second row and beyond.

Mr Cray was gesturing frantically from backstage. The twizzling of his fingers seemed to be indicating that Frankie should turn round.

Frankie stood, and with a deliberate movement swung a hand round behind himself and planted it on his rear end, partly obscuring the parting of the seams. He turned and saw the sea of faces, wide eyes, jaws sagging. Then someone laughed, and soon everyone had joined in.

All of this could only have taken a split second, but it seemed as if time had slowed down, Frankie's exposed fundament causing a rift in the space-time continuum.

"So..." he said, departing from their carefully prepared script as the laughter subsided a little. "You see... erm... you should never give in to bullies."

With a flourish of the hand, he bowed deep, only as he did so realising what a view he was giving to those behind him and backstage.

"Off!" hissed Mr Cray, and Frankie sidled off the stage, while laughter and jeers surged around the hall.

"I suppose you thought that was funny, Finnegan," said his teacher, as the others struggled to pick up their places and continue with the assembly.

Well actually, Frankie *did* think it must have been rather amusing for those in the audience. And the laughter... you can't argue with the punters.

But equally, he knew better than to argue with a teacher whose ears have gone pink and whose left eyelid is twitching with suppressed rage.

Frankie smiled sweetly instead. "Sir, sorry, sir," he said. "I had no idea, sir."

Mr Cray shook his head. "You can have another demerit for this, Finnegan." Which meant Frankie had accumulated three now, which meant detention tomorrow.

"Sir?" said Frankie.

Mr Cray raised an eyebrow above his twitching eye.

"My trousers, sir?"

He sent Frankie to the central office, where the smiling secretary whose name Frankie could never remember did her best to stitch up the seat of his trousers while Frankie sat by the window with his blazer over his lap to protect his modesty.

There were lots of smirks and comments when Frankie went into the science lab for the first lesson of the day. He was used to that kind of thing, though. He knew how to deflect the abuse by joining in with the jokes, riding the punches.

"Hey, big boy. Burst any trousers lately?"

He smiled. He grinned. He said, "Only one pair today. I'm doing okay."

"Does my bum look big in this, Frankie?"

"Not as big as mine."

"Hey, Frankie! Show us yer kacks!"

At morning break, he went to the toilet, shut himself in a cubicle and sat down on the toilet lid with his head in his hands.

Back in the summer, he'd been on a counselling course about his weight. They'd told him about the dangers of obesity: diabetes, heart problems, strokes, having to shop for clothes from special catalogues for the over-sized. They'd shown him pictures of extra-large people: a woman who took up an entire park bench, a man emerging from a pool who had a huge round belly and man-boobs like beachballs. They'd told him about healthy eating and exercise and the importance of keeping up the new regime.

He'd stopped off for a pizza and chips on the way home. Hungry work, being counselled.

He rubbed at his face and straightened.

On the back of the cubicle door someone had scrawled a poem:

There was a young boy called Fatty Finnegan
He ate all the pies in the kitchen bin again
He burst his pants when he breathed in again
Poor old Fatty he'll never be thin again

That had been fast work.

The bell went for end of break.

Frankie didn't move. From his porcelain throne he could hear the rush of people in the corridor outside: people shouting and laughing, footsteps squeaking on the wooden floor, the background murmur of voices and feet.

The noise died down, and then all was silence.

The door went and someone came into the boys' toilets. Frankie closed his eyes and pictured Mr Cray prowling for skivers, a fierce black sniffer dog straining at the leash. If they caught Frankie, they'd put him in the cage again, and hoist it up the flagpole on the greensward in front of Mr Grimes' office. It wouldn't be the first time. They liked to make an example of the fat ones like Frankie. It was that kind of school.

Frankie raised his feet off the floor.

He heard the steady stream of liquid on liquid in the next cubicle, and then the clatter of the door as his neighbour left without flushing. Soon Frankie was alone again.

They'd had a careers session earlier in the week, run by an adviser from the local Careers Service. She'd asked the class if they knew what they wanted to do when they left school. About half had put their hands in the air, including Frankie.

Marji Singh wanted to be a beautician, which was fortunate for her as the local college offered courses. Harry Barker wanted to join the army, with the ultimate aim of getting into the SAS. Wookie Trew didn't really know, but definitely wanted to go to university to study social sciences.

"Yes?" said the adviser, turning her patient smile towards Frankie. "What is it that you're hoping to do?"

Frankie hesitated. "Well," he said, "I know I've set my sights high, but there's nothing wrong with ambition, as the Chihuahua said to the Great Dane."

"Yes?"

"Well, it's my greatest desire to become a professional footballer."

It had been fascinating to see her expression shift as she tried to work out how to break the news that, no matter how good their ball control, fat kids can't run.

Now, Frankie knew that had been a mistake. He no longer

expected to play for Chelsea as a holding midfielder. He belonged in a freak show.

He had a wonderful picture book somewhere in one of the stacks of books in his bedroom, called something like *Circus of Horrors*, crammed full of old black and white images of what the Victorians had called not "freaks" but "human prodigies".

Chang Woo Gow was a Chinese giant who had toured Britain in the late nineteenth century before settling down with his English wife and children to run a teashop in Bournemouth. Commodore Nutt was a dwarf performer otherwise known as "the thirty-thousand dollar Nutt". And who could forget Lady Euphemia-Eugenie, the two-headed woman who could swallow a coin with one mouth and spit it out of the other?

They could add to that cast list, Bountiful Frankie, The Boy Who Last Saw His Own Feet Ten Years Ago. He could sit on a specially designed extra-large chaise-longue in a booth of his own, and people would pay to come in and feed him doughnuts. They could have a Guess The Weight competition. One ton or two?

You could keep your bearded ladies and cannonball dwarves: *everyone* would be queuing up to see The Boy Who.

For a long time, Frankie was no longer in a cramped cubicle with smells of bleach and bodily functions. Instead, he was reclining in his booth, with smells of sawdust and performing animals, and the jangling music of the travelling fun fair all around him. This was Faraway, the world of his daydreams, his escape from the real world. In Faraway he could be whoever he wanted to be. He could be Two-Ton Frankie, overflowing his chaise-longue, or he could be Fast Frankie, school athlete and best friend of everyone.

In Faraway, he could relax. He didn't have to worry about going home and discovering whatever mad thing his mother had done today. He didn't have to worry about the fights between Mother and Father, which carried on even though they didn't live in the same house any more. He didn't have to contend with the blanket of gloom that had settled over his home ever since the perfect daughter had died in a tragic accident two years before.

In Faraway, everything was okay.

Faraway was *Frankie*'s world.

The bell again. Voices and feet in the corridor. Kids bashing in through the toilet doors, yelling and arguing. Toilets flushing, taps and hand-driers roaring.

Lunchtime already.

Frankie took a leak, flushed, and emerged from his cubicle. He washed his hands, wiped them on the not-quite-good-as-new seat of his trousers and went out to face the normal world again.

Lunch helped. Pizza, chips and crisps, sitting with Wookie, who was far too nice to remind Frankie of his bum-baring humiliation in front of the masses. Wookie wasn't his real name, but it had stuck because he was the hairiest kid in Year 10 – even hairier than Lucy Brakes – and everyone thought he looked like Chewbacca out of *Star Wars*; and anyway, he liked "Wookie" better than his real name, which was Keith.

"So," said Wookie, through a mouthful of burger. "You suddenly find out you're the new ruler of the world. You can do what you want. You even have power over the fabric of the universe itself. So what are the first three things you do?"

"I'd make changes," said Frankie.

"What kind of changes?"

"I'd change it all. I'd change every last thing."

"Okay," said Wookie. "That's number one. What are the other two things you'd do?"

Frankie thought longer this time. "I'd probably change it all back again after that," he said.

Wookie nodded. "And third?"

"Bigger pizzas," said Frankie. "Most definitely, bigger pizzas."

3. The Owner's Representative

The next morning Frankie woke to the creaking of the pub sign outside his window. He rolled over, planted his feet on the floor and stood. *The Circus of Horrors* lay on the floor. There wasn't a Two Ton Kid in there along with Chang Woo Gow, Commodore Nutt and Lady Euphemia-Eugenie. He'd looked.

He went across to the window and peered outside. There really was a pea-souper this morning. The fog was so thick that everything he could see seemed closer: the pub sign, the street lamps, the houses squeezed together across the street.

He washed at the sink in the corner, then dressed and went downstairs. In the kitchen he made peanut butter and jam sandwiches, and a large chocolate shake.

No sign of Mother. She had been drinking her medicinal milk last night. He could tell from the unwashed glass, and the brandy bottle still out on the side.

When he left for school, she was at the top of the stairs.

"I'll be late back this afternoon," he called up to her. "We have to sand the giant again. You know how it is."

The air was heavy with cold moisture, and the scent of something salty, of the sea. Frankie could barely see the far side of the road now. He crossed carefully, listening out for any traffic and being careful not to slip on the damp cobbles.

For a long time he appeared to be the only person heading to school this morning, then he heard the sound of a bicycle and Barking passed him, struggling up the hill on what looked like a miniature penny farthing.

Frankie headed up the steep steps of the Drop, pausing part way for breath. At the top he turned left and then, at the junction with Crestfallen Street, he went into the corner shop.

At first, he didn't notice anything different, but then he realised that the pale, thin, dark-haired girl at the till was not Cindy. He couldn't remember the last time he had been in here and had not been served by Cindy.

He took a king-sized Mars bar and a packet of smoky bacon crisps and reached into his pocket for the money.

She looked like Cindy, though.

A bit thinner. And her hair wasn't quite so punk, her make-up less harsh, and with comic pink circles on her cheeks like an old-fashioned china doll.

Her eyes looked at Frankie, then switched to look down at the items he had placed on the counter. "That will be..." She spoke mechanically, and as she paused Frankie almost believed that he could hear a whirring of cogs and gears. "...Eight-y... sev-en... pence, please." She put a hand out, flipped it palm-up and uncoiled the fingers, awaiting his money.

He gave her a pound coin.

"Thank you. You have tendered... one... pound... only."

The till jangled open, the hand jerked over and dropped the coin in the correct slot. With a few more mechanical movements, the new Cindy took his change and swung back to hand it to him.

"Your change is... thir-teen pence." The hand swivelled, the coins slid off and Frankie caught them. "Have a nice day... sir."

The head dipped and the eyes fixed themselves on a magazine lying open on the counter. Apparently, a wealthy movie star had just bought a new house in the south of France.

Frankie stared at her expressionless face, and the absolutely motionless way she held her body.

He left the shop and continued on his way.

School happened.

Frankie put up with the "see the fat kid" stares, the giggles and the comments about his trouser-splittingly good performance in yesterday's assembly. He grinned and smiled and laughed a lot.

He daydreamed a lot, too, staring into space and changing everything.

He got through.

Last lesson of the day, last lesson of the week. Frankie stared at the clock on the wall by the classroom door.

Ten more minutes of French and then the weekend.

Madame Gilbert was talking, but her words were little more than an insect buzz in his ear. He could hear the clock ticking loudly over her drone. He could see its mechanism, all cogs and springs twisting and ratcheting along in the glass casement below the clock face.

"*Ecoutez vous*, Frankie? Are you listening?"

He looked at her. He sensed his brain working like the mechanism of the clock on the wall, only not quite so well wound up. "*Oui, Madame*," he assured her.

She narrowed her eyes and opened her mouth to say something. She was going to test him, find out exactly what he had heard and what he had missed.

She shook her head. It was Friday, nearly time to go. She turned away from Frankie, and returned to addressing the whole class. "I want all of page 40 done by Tuesday, okay?"

Afterwards, Frankie trudged along the corridor and down a flight of stairs to his form room, where Mr Cray would be supervising detention.

Frankie went in and sat at a desk at the front of the class.

There were two others here today: Harry Barker and a blonde girl from Year 9 whose name he didn't know.

"Okay, Barking?" said Frankie.

"Hey, Fatagain. What you doin'?" said Barker. "Is it cos you's fat?"

The girl snorted a laugh, and Frankie joined in.

Ruler of the World, first thing he'd do: change Harry Barker.

The board on the wall was black, with a little shelf beneath where someone had propped a wooden-handled blackboard rubber and a few short pieces of chalk. Frankie wondered where the whiteboard had gone.

He looked out of the window at the retreating backs of all those whose weekend had already begun. Thin winter sunlight cast a yellowish veil over the scene, the air wavering. Frankie wondered if the fog was returning or if this was just some kind of trick of the light.

Oddly, he felt peaceful, as if a weight was starting to lift. He rolled his shoulders.

Barking was muttering something to the girl, but Frankie didn't care.

Mr Cray entered the room, wearing a long-tailed jacket and carrying a stick – a cane! He had mutton-chop whiskers, which he had not had this morning, and under his arm he had a large, leather-bound ledger, which he placed on his desk with a thud.

He rapped the book with a knuckle. "Barker, Finnegan, Strachan. You all have entries in the Ledger of Misdemeanours."

He opened the book, and ran a finger down rows of tiny copperplate handwriting.

He stopped, with a finger pointing at one entry. "Barker," he said. "Disobedience, insubordination, slovenly presentation of self, cycling on the pavement."

Barking stared at their teacher. "I –"

"And answering back!" snapped Mr Cray. "Stand."

Barking stood.

"Hand out. No: palm up."

He did so.

Mr Cray brought the cane down sharply on Harry Barker's hand.

Barking snatched his hand away with a yelp and held it to his chest, eyeing Mr Cray in disbelief.

"Hand out."

Slowly, Barking put his hand back out and held it trembling in mid-air between himself and the teacher.

The cane cracked down again.

This time, Barking held his hand in place, eyes brimming with tears.

Again.

Mr Cray returned to the Ledger of Misdemeanours.

"Finnegan," he said, finding his place again.

Strangely, Frankie still felt calm. He had been here before. *Tom Brown's Schooldays. Jennings Goes to School. Just William.* All in the pages of his books, all in his head, in some faraway place. "Sir?" he said.

"Unauthorised absence from lessons. Indecent exposure of undergarments in school assembly. That's three lashes for you, too. Stand and put your hand out."

Frankie stood, but didn't put his hand forward. "Sir," he said, in a low voice, "I think you'll recall that I have already been punished."

Confusion clouded the teacher's face. "I..."

"I have already been punished and no further action is required."

"I..." Mr Cray looked at the big ledger again, and then back at Frankie. "Sit," he said, and Frankie returned to his seat.

Frankie didn't really understand, except... this was like sitting in his window watching imaginary coaches go by, like hiding in the toilets and imagining himself in the freak show.

Frankie *knew* this world. It was *his.*

Mr Cray ran his finger down the entries in the ledger again. He stopped, and said, "Strachan."

Frankie glanced across.

Barking sat clutching his hand to his chest, still managing to keep the tears from running down his cheeks, but only just. The girl, Wotsit Strachan, cowered back in her seat, staring at Mr Cray.

"Confronting your superiors with a funny look in your eye,"

said Mr Cray. "And opening a packet of crisps at the wrong end." He sucked air between his teeth. "Serious," he said. "Very serious."

Frankie cleared his throat, and when Mr Cray looked across Frankie gave a little shake of the head. "You've already punished her, too, Mr Cray, sir," he said.

Mr Cray looked back at the ledger and nodded.

He turned, took the blackboard rubber and began to wipe at a perfectly clean area of the board. "Very well," he said. "Dismissed."

They filed out of the room.

The corridor was long and narrow, with dark wood panelling. Gas lamps were distributed along one wall, each burning low, contributing a dim glow to fend off the gloom. Photographs hung in frames, large groups of pupils in high collars and stripy blazers, their teachers with waxed moustaches and straw boaters.

The Strachan girl ran for the door, but Harry Barker stopped and turned, confronting Frankie. He gripped him by a handful of shirt at his throat and forced him against the wall.

"I don't know what's going on," he hissed, his eyes flicking from side to side. "And I don't know what you're doing. But..."

He had lost the thread. Too confused.

"You're not to tell anyone, you understand? About what went on in there."

Frankie shrugged. What was he going to tell anyone, anyway? He remained leaning against the wall as Barking turned and hurried away after the girl.

Mr Cray came out a few seconds later.

"Mr Cray, sir," said Frankie.

His teacher looked at him, as if puzzled. "What's happening?" Mr Cray asked. He looked both ways along the corridor. "Where is this place?"

"I don't know, Mr Cray, sir. But I think it's far away."

Frankie headed outside. The main school block was a Victorian red-brick building, with a narrow strip of garden set in front of it, and then the main playground with newer buildings off that. Frankie stopped in the playground and looked back.

An empty cage, large enough for two or three people was suspended from a flagpole where the school flag should have been.

He shook his head and turned.

The main path took him out to Hall Lane, which ran along the crest of the hill facing the bay. He headed down a steep cobbled road towards the promenade. The guesthouses here all had "Vacancies" signs in their windows, as they would all winter, and many of the shops had shutters pulled down, closed for the off-season.

Things seemed pretty normal here.

Frankie realised he was worried. Scared, even. He had always had a vivid imagination – one of the kinder things his mother called him was Faraway Frankie, because he was always daydreaming.

But... well, there had been *boundaries*. He had known the difference between grim reality and those times when he was escaping within. But today... things were leaking.

He stopped before a lamp post, shorter than the modern ones, and cast from iron painted black. The light itself was encased in uneven glass, which held a delicate brass mechanism to control the flow of gas.

He concentrated.

The post was metal, tall, and the light itself was encased in translucent plastic. That was better. That was real.

Frankie took a side alley between jostling houses, heading down the steps to the prom. He came out between two beach huts. The bay curved round to either side, and the prom, with its fringe of beach huts extended almost as far as the eye could see. Off to the left, the pier thrust out into the bay, a long line like half a bridge with buildings on top: the amusements, the cafés, the theatre, the lifeboat station way out at the end. Frankie blinked. The pier looked longer from this perspective. He was used to looking down on it from the Drop.

Frankie went over to the cast iron railing and looked out across the bay. The sea was calm, the low tide exposing weed-covered rocks and beyond them, an expanse of flat, glistening mud. There were footprints out there, like perforations across the surface. Someone must have been out digging for fishing bait: lugworms and ragworms and the great poisonous devil's tail worms which could, according to local legend, suck a grown man beneath the mud.

Frankie set off towards the pier.

The beach huts were painted in yellows, blues and reds, the colours faded by sunlight and the battering of salty sea winds. Heavy padlocks and shutters across the windows secured them for the winter. From September to April the town went into hibernation, the guesthouses empty, the entertainments closed down, half of the shops boarded up.

Even the pier was mostly closed down at this time of year, other than the amusement arcade Frankie's father tended, and the chip shop by the pier entrance.

Frankie went in through the door of Fast Fries, and was immediately struck by hot air, heavy with the smells of old cooking oil and batter and fish. "Large chips and a battered saveloy, please, Mr Singh," said Frankie.

Mr Singh turned to the rack where the chips were draining and thrust a scoop into them. With a sharp swivel at the waist and a flip of the wrist, he tipped them into a polystyrene container, then reached for some more. Switching to a pair of tongs, he caught the sausage and dropped it on the chips, and then deftly folded everything inside two layers of paper.

"That will be..." he said, and Frankie was suddenly reminded of the new Cindy in the corner shop this morning. "Two pounds and... eighty... pence, please."

Mr Singh put a hand out, and flipped it palm upwards.

Frankie peered into his lifeless eyes and said, "Twelve squid past the octopus, I think."

Mr Singh didn't flicker. He stood with his hand out, awaiting Frankie's money.

Frankie dropped three pounds onto his palm.

"You have tendered... three... pounds... only."

Mr Singh sprung the till and dropped the coins into their rightful place. Change in hand, he swung back towards Frankie and said, "Your change is... twenty... pence."

"That's okay," said Frankie, backing away with his food. "You keep the change, Mr Singh."

"Your change is... twenty... pence."

Frankie backed through the doors and emerged on the wide paved area at the head of the pier.

A muffled voice followed him: "Your change is... twenty... pence."

Frankie turned.

The entrance to the pier was before him, posters and bright colours and banners vying for his attention.

Dodgems. Have your palm read. Tattooist. Free entry! Big cash prizes. Maxx game here! Grab for fun: soft toys and more. Deep sea aquarium. Kids ride free. Refreshments... ices... candy floss... all day diner...

Frankie pushed through the swing doors with one hand, clutching his sausage and chips to his chest with the other.

He heard jangling bells and fun fair music, voices raised from somewhere further out, distant hammering, the throb of a generator.

This part of the pier was all under cover and was the only part that stayed even partly open during the off season. Even so, much was closed.

The dodgems were to his left, all parked up in the centre of their circuit for the winter. To his right, the Gypsy Queen's palm-reading booth was boarded up, as was the entrance to the tattoo parlour.

One day years ago, Frankie's father had gone in there on a quiet day and had the name "Stella" tattooed on his left buttock. He had thought this a grandly romantic gesture, but Frankie's mother – the Stella in question – had cursed him, saying she didn't want to be sat on all day long, thank you very much.

Next along was the amusements hall, the largest enclosed space here other than the theatre and the dodgems. Gaming machines lined the walls, and more stood in ranks between them, all packed as densely as they could possibly manage.

One-armed bandits stood with levers ready to pull, buttons to push, flashing instructions telling you to hold, push, nudge, start over. Bar football tables stood unused, all the little men at different angles. Video game machines stood with laser guns dangling from chains, joy sticks, steering wheels and other controls lined up before huge screens.

The machines sang to Frankie. Bells and whistles, electronic chirruping, voices saying "Shoot" and "Play now" and "Gooooaaaaaal!"

No sign of Father.

Frankie finished his saveloy and wiped his hand on his trousers. He wandered around the arcade, mesmerised by the flashing lights and noise.

He came out into daylight a short time later, blinking, reaching automatically for the wire bin by the doorway to deposit his chip paper.

The bare boards of the pier stretched out into the bay before him. He could barely see the lifeboat station at the far end. It wasn't *usually* that far away.

He looked down and saw the sea through gaps between the boards.

Between Frankie and the end of the pier a lot of new activity was taking place. Gangs of workers erected new rides, along with more covered areas and buildings, extending the sheltered section of the pier further out along its length into the sea.

Frankie looked past this, towards the pier's end. It was as if a new section had been inserted into the pier to accommodate this new development, or as if the pier had somehow been stretched to make room.

He would come back at the weekend for a closer look, but now it was getting late. The light was closing in, and another sea fog was floating in across the bay.

Frankie turned back through the doorway to the main covered walkway, the aquarium with its Thrills Of The Deep on his right and the amusement arcade to his left. A row of cut-out figures with holes where their faces should be stood by the entrance: a deep-sea diver, a strong man, a bathing belle, a big gorilla complete with shiny fake fur. In his bedroom, Frankie had a photo of himself peering out of the strong man's face-hole. Narrow waist, upside-down triangular torso, rippling muscles in the arms and across the shoulders. Frankie with a perfect physique. Far easier than dieting and exercise.

The lights on a row of machines along the back wall of the arcade flashed out, and some of the jingles and sound effects cut off in mid-burst. Another row went out, and Frankie spotted his father working his way through the arcade, cutting the power for the night.

"Father."

His father looked up, then hurried across.

"Frankie, my boy," he said, putting a hand on Frankie's arm and trying to steer him away from the arcade. "What you doing here, then? I'm just closing up." He patted a metal box strung from a strap across his shoulders. "I got the day's takings in here and I'm just waiting for the Owner to come, then I'm off."

The Owner. Frankie had never seen the Owner, but everyone knew of him. He ran most of the town and people seemed to be both grateful that someone employed them and just a little wary of someone with so much power.

Just then a voice called out from the far end of the arcade. "Finnegan?"

Frankie's father pushed at him now, and said, "Get along, son. I'll see you later, maybe."

Frankie allowed himself to be directed towards the exit. Out in the main through-walk again, he ducked behind one of the cut-outs – the strong man. Frankie wanted to see what the Owner looked like.

He peered back out of the face-hole and saw that his father had returned to cutting the power to his machines.

Another figure appeared, coming from the pier end of the arcade. It was a man: short and thin, in a suit that was a size too big. He looked only a few years older than Frankie himself. He had a thin scar on one jaw, and a cold look in his grey eyes – making him seem even more lifeless than chip-shop Mr Singh and not-Cindy from the corner shop. Franmie found it hard to believe this could be the Owner.

"Mickey," the man said, and Frankie's father came out to join him in one of the arcade's entrance arches. "How's business, Mickey?"

Frankie's father was squinting at him. "Oh, it's you," he said. "I was expecting the Owner."

"Mickey," said the youngster in the big suit. "Calm yourself. The Owner sends his regards."

"Where is he?"

"He's safe," said the young man. "He's being taken care of."

Frankie ducked his head back down, just as his father's visitor started to peer around.

"You know me," the voice said, getting closer. "I'm the Owner's representative. You'll be dealing with me from now on."

Suddenly, a head loomed in the face-hole directly above Frankie, and light glinted off cold grey eyes.

Then the head was gone again. Frankie was okay: he hadn't been spotted.

"You've got a nice set-up here," said the Owner's representative. "Even if it smells of chips. You could be replaced easy enough. You understand? Now where's the takings?"

Frankie heard a metallic sound which he thought was the money box being placed on a surface, or opened.

"Not good," said the Owner's representative. "Not good."

"It's winter," said Frankie's father. "You can see for yourself. The place is deserted."

"Not good," said the voice again. "We like you, Mickey. We don't want to lose you. But..."

After a long silence Frankie saw in the reflections on the wall that lights were going out across the way again. Cautiously, he peered out through the strong man's face. His father was alone, working his way around the arcade.

Frankie came back out and stood in one of the entrance archways.

"You still here?" said his father, when he noticed Frankie standing there. "Come on, let's be off."

Together, they walked back up the pier and out through the swing doors.

"What was that about?" asked Frankie.

His father hesitated, then said, "Business. Just business."

"What was that about the Owner? They're 'taking care of him'. What does that mean? Sounds like they've got him locked up, or worse."

"What he said. That's all," said Frankie's father. "No one wants any harm to come to the Owner. Place'd fall apart. There's been some strange goings on lately. Maybe the Owner's losing his grip – that'd be why they're taking care of him."

"It's not surprising he's losing it if he's being 'taken care of' by people like that," said Frankie.

"You don't want the Owner to lose his grip, son. Oh no. Like

I say: he loses his grip and the whole damn show falls apart."

They came to a flight of steps which led up through a row of shops to Sea View Parade.

"You calling in tonight, Dad?"

His father gave a small shake of the head. "Perhaps not," he said. "You know how it is."

4. Tiddley Om Pom Pom

Back at home, puffed from the climb up the steep streets and alleys of his home town, Frankie paused on the front doorstep.

He turned his key in the lock, went inside and stooped to remove his shoes and place them in the shoe basket. He smoothed his hair in the mirror.

Just then, he noticed that the heavy door to the front room was half-open. Remembering the strange footprints yesterday, he went through. The room was dark, its heavy velvet drapes cutting out the streetlight. An oil lamp burnt on the mantelpiece, glinting off brass ornaments and shining in the dark wood panelling of the room.

Frankie turned to the Shrine to Grace, as he thought of it. On the dark sideboard he saw a vase of dried flowers and grasses, an empty checkerboard-patterned fruit bowl, an unlit cream-coloured candle in a brass holder, and a single sepia-tinted family photograph showing young Frankie and Grace with their parents. All the usual photographs, the conch shell, the ribbon and the other mementoes... gone.

He left the room, automatically pulling the door closed behind him. Then, remembering it had been open, he paused and pushed the door ajar again.

Mother was in the kitchen, using a long-handled feather duster to flick at cobwebs where the wall met the ceiling. She was wearing a colourful flowery jacket Frankie hadn't seen before, and a white apron.

"Frankie!" she said, when he came in. She put the duster down, stepped towards him and planted a big dry kiss on his cheek. "How was your day, Frankie?"

Frankie stared at her.

For two years she had resisted any kind of change in the house and now... well, things were different.

"I'd give it six out of ten, Mother," he said. Then, remembering that the day had actually been a bit different to the norm, he corrected himself: "Perhaps six and a half."

She returned to her dusting.

"I like the jacket," said Frankie. "Is it new?" He couldn't quite picture Mother shopping for clothes. She bought everything mail order, so perhaps this had come from a catalogue too.

"New, dear? I've had it years, you UGL."

"Where are all the photos?" Frankie asked. "From the front room... the sideboard."

Mother glanced back at him. "Photographs?" she said. "What do you mean: photographs? There's that one of us all at Blackpool. So nice to holiday by the sea, don't you think?"

Frankie watched her, flicking at the same corner with her duster until a single strand of dusty grey spider silk came away. She was either being deliberately difficult, or this was just one of her more erratic days. He couldn't decide which.

But he liked it.

He noticed then that there was nothing on the stove. Mother nearly always had the evening meal bubbling away to mush by this time.

"What's for tea?" he asked.

She beamed. "I thought we could get fish and chips from Fred's Plaice," she said. She put a hand to his cheek. "It was your birthday yesterday, after all. We should celebrate."

When Frankie got back from the chip shop the two of them had tea, and later Frankie watched his DVD of *The Hound of the Baskervilles* in a room lit by candles and oil lamps. It seemed just right.

He went to bed, tired and satisfied, feeling as if things were running his way for once.

Frankie woke in the depth of the night: the kind of time that hasn't made its mind up whether to be very late or very early.

He could hear rain steadily pounding on the roof and the street, and running water from where the guttering was blocked over his window and overflowed onto the pavement below.

Thunder rumbled, followed by a deep groaning sound, unlike anything Frankie had heard before: so deep he could feel it vibrating through his bed frame. He wondered whether it might be a small earth tremor, but Frankie had read about earthquakes and knew they were different to this: a more definite shaking, lasting a few seconds and then stopping; this was longer and less shaky than he would have expected. A short time later he heard the sound again, as if giants were rearranging their furniture. Maybe the legendary Chang Woo Gow was reorganising his tea shop in Bournemouth.

Frankie dozed, dreaming of giants and two-headed ladies and performing dogs, all arguing about the arrangement of the three-piece suite.

In the morning, he peered out of his bedroom window. There was no fog today, or if there had been Frankie had slept in long enough for the winter sun to have burned it off.

The cracks between the cobbles were still wet, and puddles gathered along the side of the street, but otherwise, beneath a pale blue seaside sky, it looked like being a lovely day. Frankie decided to go down to the beach in what remained of the morning. Maybe Barking and Stu and the others would be hanging out at the skateboard park, and he could join them, just like old times, and watch them with their tricks.

Mother would no doubt remind him about his homework, but that could wait until about 11 on Sunday night, as usual. That was his most productive time, he always assured her.

He pulled on a pair of combat pants and a baggy green T-shirt and went downstairs to the first floor landing.

He stopped, wondering what was different.

The attic... He'd always wanted a room up in the attic and... and now he had it. The attic bedroom.

He'd nagged Father for years to have the roof-space converted.

He couldn't remember when this had been done, but clearly it had. Something had changed but also... it felt as if the house had been this way forever.

He passed the room that had been Grace's, the door firmly shut, as always. He wondered if Mother's transformation of the day before extended to his sister's room, too: had she been in and finally put his sister's things away into storage?

He didn't look. He went downstairs, instead, lured by the smell of frying bacon and toast.

Mother greeted him with a smile. "Breakfast?" she asked, as he seated himself at the kitchen table.

He pushed a used plate and cutlery away to make room for those his mother brought over to him.

She nodded. "Yes, your father said to say 'good morning', but he was up and out early today. He said it was going to be a good day at the arcade, he could feel it in his water."

Frankie stared at her.

He pronged a button mushroom with his fork, brought it to his mouth, bit.

"Nice mushrooms," he said.

Which seemed to say it all, really.

Outside, he walked down the road towards the prom.

After a couple of minutes he stopped in the middle of the street and looked all around. The rows of terraced houses had become taller than before, some of them three or four storeys high, and they huddled closer together, leaning in over the street as if they were trying to meet those opposite.

Today, everything was squashed closer together, houses

leaning at all kinds of interesting angles, cobbled streets snaking down the steep hill towards the sea.

Frankie remembered the groaning sounds in the night. Furniture moving on a grand scale.

He turned into an alleyway that was barely wider than his shoulders. A black iron rail was attached to one wall, and he clung to this as he descended, the ground here still slick from the night's rain.

He came out by Buckets And Spades and saw that the boards had been taken down, the shop open for weekend trade. His first thought was that that was rather optimistic of the owners, but then he took in the sight of the promenade and realised they had it entirely right.

The prom was busy today. Couples strolled arm in arm, with parasols to shelter them from the unseasonal sunshine. Children darted about, chasing hoops with sticks or after scruffy dogs on long leashes. Elderly people stood at the iron railing above the beach, or sat on the ornate benches, some eating ice creams in huge cones.

A group of kids of about Frankie's age had gathered outside the Blue Lagoon dance hall, anonymous in their hoodies and baggy jeans, some with skateboards over their shoulders, some swigging from cans of Diamond White. A girl of similar age stood nearby, as if uncertain whether or not to join the group. As Frankie watched, she turned away and headed down the steps to the beach instead.

Down on the beach, the tide was halfway. Small children queued up with their parents for rides on blinkered, straw-hatted donkeys. Trailers had been pulled down into the water, little cabins on wheels where ladies could change into swimming costumes and descend into the water unobserved.

Somewhere nearby, a brass band struck up, and something about its oompah style made Frankie briefly dizzy so that he had to catch himself against the wall to stop from falling.

A jangling of bells caught his attention. They were attached to the ankles and wrists of a cartwheeling woman, who rolled past trailing streamers of gauzy material in pink and powder blue. Sprinting after her, a dwarf waved a placard over his head:

COME TO FARAWAY PIER
LOTS OF NEW ATTRACTIONS
FREE ENTRY!!!

Frankie was heading for the pier in any case. He wanted to find his father. He wanted to see if *he* had changed, too.

He kept on having to sidestep and pause as he made headway in the jostling crowd. He had to remind himself that this was a weekend in dreary, grim November, and not a spring bank holiday.

No: even spring bank holidays weren't usually this busy.

He paused on the circular turning area before the entrance to the pier, glancing in to Fast Fries but not seeing Mr Singh today.

Newly painted in red and gold, on boards two metres high stretched across above the pier entrance, were the words "Faraway Pier".

Posters were stuck to every available surface. New attractions: watch the performing monkeys; see Master Huff the amazing ventriloquist (you'll really believe a brush can speak); spy on the mermaid at the deep sea aquarium; watch Henry the Horse dancing the waltz; jugglers, fire-eaters, pierrots, the bearded lady and her moustachioed maidens; the ghost train and the tunnel of love; plus all your old favourites.

Frankie pushed in through the swing doors and was struck by a barrage of noise: voices, music, gaming machines, engines.

He walked on past the dodgems and the arcade and out onto the first open stretch of the pier.

It was wide here, the tarred boards bleached white by the sun and salt. A short distance away, the new attractions had been completed now, and there were rides and stalls, and large areas covered by striped canopies.

Beyond... Frankie couldn't see the end of the pier, it was too far away.

He turned back under cover, and stepped through one of the entrance arches into the arcade. It was even noisier here, if possible. Groups stood around the machines, hauling on the levers and thumping at the buttons. They cheered whenever coins jangled out in a torrent for collection; they groaned when the third cherry *just* flipped over and became a lemon and the money was lost.

Business was good today. Frankie hoped this meant his father wouldn't have any more trouble with the Owner's representative over low takings.

After a few minutes, he spotted his father.

He looked harassed. He was scurrying about between the machines, as if waiting for something to go wrong. Whenever he found a vacant machine, he tapped someone on the shoulder and gestured and they would smile and talk, move into the spare slot and start feeding the machine coins.

Frankie threaded his way through the arcade until he caught up with his father.

"Father," he said. "Busy today, isn't it?"

The small man looked up, glanced away, then looked at Frankie again.

"Frankie," he said. "Hmm? Oh yes. Busy. Very busy. Can't stop. Don't want to disappoint the Owner. Have to please him. He doesn't want to lose me, you know."

As he spoke, he walked, occasionally kicking at a machine that had stuck, or guiding someone to the lever to set it going.

Frankie looked at the people playing the machines. They were transfixed, intent on only one thing: feeding the ravenous gaming machines with coin after coin after coin.

"Who exactly is this Owner?" Frankie asked his father, as he pursued him along the rows. "What does he own?"

His father squinted at him. "He owns everything," he said, surprised. "This place, this town, me, you, *them*... the whole shebang."

Frankie stopped, allowing his father to continue on his way.

This was Faraway, the place of his daydreams.

Things were different here. Maybe someone should tell the Owner about that.

Frankie looked around. With business this good, the arcade could do with an extension. He peered at the far wall and blinked, and saw that it wasn't really a wall, more a partition, a flimsy divider...

...and it was gone and the arcade extended out into another row of machines. The extension must jut out over the water, he realised. He hoped the supports were good, but he knew they would be. This pier had already been expanding: a bit of extra width wouldn't do any harm.

Frankie smiled.

His father was over on the far side now, guiding punters towards the newly available machines. These machines were hungry, like new-born babies. They hadn't been fed at all yet. They needed attention.

Back on the prom in the heat of the early afternoon, Frankie strolled, soaking up the atmosphere and sucking candy floss from a stick for his lunch.

This stretch of the prom was where the high street came down to the waterfront and shops and cafés were lined up before the bay. Stalls had been set up along the prom here, so that there were traders and entertainers vying for attention from all sides.

Ahead, the prom turned sharply inland to wrap around the town's small harbour. Yachts crowded in there, moored to floating walkways, their rigging clanking in the breeze.

On a grassy area, a small booth stood upright. Its walls were painted in red and white stripes, and at the front there was a curtained opening, with miniature columns to either side, painted to look like a small theatre stage. A board across the top said that this was Doctor Twizzle's Punch and Judy Extravaganza.

Quite a crowd had built up already.

Frankie approached the scene, attracted by the jaunty tune playing on the reed pipes.

By the booth, a man in grey top hat, long frock coat and checkered trousers stood, chatting with families at the front.

Frankie spotted that girl again, the one he had seen when he first reached the prom today. She looked about fourteen or fifteen and was very slight, with long dark hair that didn't look as if it had been brushed – or even washed – for at least a week. In fact her hair reminded him of the tangles of seaweed you would find along the foot of the pier at low tide. She wore a polka dot dress which looked similarly uncared for. She was wriggling her bare toes in the grass and just at that moment she looked so – *liberated* – that Frankie wanted to kick off his shoes and share the feeling.

The pipes worked into a crescendo just then, and the top-hatted man rapped several times on a small hand-held drum. He bowed low, and his hat fell off onto the grass, eliciting a torrent of giggles from small children in the front. "Ladies, gentlemen and their mums and dads," he said, in a voice that carried easily to where Frankie sat at the back. "Welcome to the one and the only Doctor Twizzle's – that's me, by the way – Doctor Twizzle's Punch and Judy Hextravaganza!"

The curtains twitched and first a long nose and then the rest of a puppet's face poked out. "It's mine!" a squeaky voice cried. "All mine! Not his at all." Again, children laughed, as much at the look on Doctor Twizzle's face as at what the puppet had said.

"Mr Punch," said the Doctor, shaking his head. "Kindly wait your turn." The puppet was really quite grotesque, from what Frankie could see, with a long nose and chin, cheeks and lips painted bright red and a conical crimson hat on its head. Its features were shiny and appeared to have been cast from clay. Everything about the puppet was exaggerated in just such a way that made it look as evil as possible.

Frankie surveyed the crowd instead. Small children loved the show, responding to every subtle change in expression on the Doctor's face, catching every joke he made as soon as he let slip the punchline. Their parents seemed hooked too, as much by the responses of their children as by the entertainment itself.

And the girl... the girl with the seaweed hair. She was transfixed, never taking her gaze off the puppets.

The play was well under way by now, and the children were into the swing of responding to Punch's taunts and jokes. When Judy left him looking after the baby and he hit it on the ground to stop it crying, he turned to the audience and squeaked, "That's the way to do it!"

Immediately, the children cried back, "That's *not* the way to do it!"

The girl just watched, a faraway look in her eyes.

A short time later, a policeman puppet tried to arrest Punch and the two exchanged blows with club and truncheon. A good swing from the policeman struck Punch on the crown of the skull and the doll's entire head shattered, exploding into a thousand tiny fragments.

The crowd gasped, and the policeman quietly said, "Ahem. I think *that*'s the way to do it."

"Behind you!" cried the children, but the policeman wouldn't look as Punch rose from the floor and swung his club down on the policeman's head.

After a long silence, Punch turned to the audience and said, "What a silly policeman! He didn't know I had a spare head..."

Frankie suddenly realised that the girl with the seaweed hair had left her place.

He swivelled and saw her slim form running away along the prom. There was something about the way she held herself as she ran... she seemed upset. He wondered what had got to her. They were only dolls, after all.

5. The Way To Do It

Frankie went after her. He wasn't sure why.

She seemed like an outsider, he supposed. Someone who didn't quite fit.

He knew what that was like.

He didn't hurry, though. It was mid-afternoon and the sun's warmth was at its peak for the day, with a slight hint of a breeze coming in from the sea. This wasn't a hurrying kind of a day.

He bought a 99 with an extra flake from one of the many stalls lining the prom and it by the Krazy Golf course, watching fathers with bright shorts and lobster-pink backs getting over-competitive as their children looked on, bemused. Hole number seven was a real swine: through the windmill and up a rutted slope which always managed to send the ball right back down to the start again no matter how hard you hit it. You had to get the ball deflected in off the corner of the windmill's base to stand a chance, Frankie knew, but he didn't tell.

There was so much going on, but Frankie was content just to stroll and soak up the atmosphere. At a coconut shy he couldn't resist the temptation, though. He plucked a ball from the rack and threw it as hard as he could. The ball struck a coconut full-on, and the nut wobbled, teetered, and then fell from its perch.

The woman at the stall cheered and gave him a big cuddly monkey. He didn't know what to do with the thing, so he sat it on a bench and waved goodbye.

He came to the pier without having seen a sign of the girl with the seaweed hair. She could be anywhere by now. He wasn't really bothered. If she mattered, she'd show up somewhere, he was sure. Faraway was that kind of place.

He considered going out onto the pier again. He could try his luck on the one-armed bandits. Judging by his performance at the coconut shy he was on a winning streak. Perhaps not, then. He wouldn't want to put a dent in Father's takings just when things were picking up again.

There were lots of new attractions on the pier, and he thought about having a closer look. The mermaid sounded interesting, and the waltzing horse. But they would be there another day.

He didn't think the girl would have gone out onto the pier.

He walked on, until he came to the Blue Lagoon dance hall. He could hear voices raised from beyond the building. A skateboard park had been built here, in the corner of what had been a car park before the steam train came to town and made cars unnecessary.

Still feeling that things were going his way, Frankie straightened his back and strode around the building to the skate park.

The gang was there: Barking and all the usual crowd. Four boys in skater get-up were going back and forth on the big half-pipe, flipping and twisting in mid-air when they hit the top of each run. Barking was with Marji Singh, leaning in close together and laughing at something. Stu and Arthur and Blunto were sharing cigarettes and cider with Jenny Pargeter and a tall red-headed girl from school whose name Frankie didn't know.

"Hey, Stu," said Frankie, joining them.

Stu looked up. "Hey, fat guy," he said. He didn't seem too pleased to see Frankie.

Frankie looked around. Great big steel waste bins taller than he was were lined up behind the Blue Lagoon, each painted with graffiti. Broken bottles lay scattered across the paving, and a rusting bike with one wheel was chained to a drainpipe. Nice place for the kids to gather.

He wasn't sure what to do. He had never quite got this hanging out thing, even though he had sometimes come along in the past with Grace. Kids standing around on street corners, or at the skateboard park... What did they actually *do?*

He stood, slightly apart from Stu and the others, hands in his pockets.

Barking broke away from Marji then, and with a sneering look at Frankie, flicked his board up into his hands with the toe of one baseball boot. He went over to the big half-pipe, stepped onto the board, and started to work up speed.

Up and down. It was all about getting your centre of gravity right, Frankie saw.

"You haven't seen a girl, have you?" he asked. "A bit shorter than me, long messy hair, looked upset."

He should have known better.

"Hey, Barking!" yelled Marji. "Frankie's got a girl!"

Frankie felt his cheeks burning, and not from the sun. "I..."

It was Stu's turn now. "Why was she upset, fat guy?" he asked. "D'you sit on her, or something?"

"Nah," said Blunto, a small kid with big ears and a face that looked like it had been ironed. "He showed her his kacks, didn't you, Finnegan? Showed her your smelly brown kacks."

"Ah, you guys," said Marji. "I think it's sweet. She's probably at the tattoo place getting your name done in a big heart on her shoulder blade. I reckon it's dead sweet."

"No..." said Frankie. "She doesn't know me, I just... she was upset and I..."

He pointed at Blunto's skateboard. "Hey," he said, "is that as easy as it looks? Like surfing, right?"

"You've been surfing?" asked Stu. Then he turned to the others and said, "Meet the world's first surfing whale."

Frankie laughed with them. "No," he said. "But I've seen it on the telly. Looks easy."

Blunto held the board towards him. "Go on then, Finnegan. You have a go. Best to start with the big half-pipe – that's easiest."

Frankie took the board. "Thank you," he said. "And thanks

for the advice."

He turned and eyed the half-pipe, where Barking was flipping and twisting like he was on invisible wires.

Things were going Frankie's way today.

This was his world, and he could make things happen, like extending Father's arcade and convincing Mr Cray not to cane him.

He placed the board, put a foot on it and pushed off with the other. It ran smoothly and in a straight line. When he leaned back it tilted and turned in that direction, so he leaned forward again to correct his line. Like he thought, just a matter of centring yourself.

He pushed a couple more times, so that he had picked up speed by the time he came in at an angle and hit the slope. He bent his knees and leaned into the incline.

Halfway up, he slowed to a halt.

He straightened a little, and felt the front of the board lifting. He twisted and the board turned.

Suddenly, he was facing down the slope again, and picking up speed.

A big cheer went up from the watching gang.

Frankie smiled and waved.

He went three-quarters of the way up this time, before straightening, twisting, and turning to face downwards again.

Another cheer.

And then a shout from much closer: "What the –!"

There was a blur in the corner of his vision, then somebody angling across in front of him.

Too late to do anything.

The borrowed board clipped the back of the other person's and went from under Frankie's feet. He flew through the air, then came down in a tangle of limbs.

Too many limbs.

Too much snarling and cursing.

There was someone underneath him.

He tried to extricate himself, but only succeeded in putting his hand in the other person's face.

He rolled over to one side, and found himself sitting on the slope. Perhaps things weren't all running his way today after all.

"And for my next trick..." he said.

Harry Barker flipped up onto all fours like an angry cat.

"Sorry, Barking," said Frankie, struggling to his feet. "I think you cut across my line."

"Finnegan..." hissed Barking.

"Perhaps we could talk about this," said Frankie. "Like gentlemen?" He thought of the Punch and Judy show then, of Punch's china head shattering into a thousand pieces. Weighing up all the available evidence, and knowing the person involved, Frankie rather suspected that he might share that fate if he allowed Barking to get his hands on him now.

"Okay," Frankie said. "I agree. Let's discuss this later."

With a toe he pushed Blunto's skateboard into the way, just as Barking stepped towards him.

Barking went down again, and Frankie took the opportunity to sidestep around the half-pipe and make for the alley by the side of the Blue Lagoon.

Glancing back, he saw that the others had gone to Barking's assistance instead of setting off in pursuit. That was good.

He emerged on the prom, the crowds as thick as before.

Just past a hot dog stall, a balloon sculptor was tying long thin balloons into the shape of a... well... a *thing*. Frankie decided not to hang around to see what the thing turned out to be.

Down on the beach, donkeys paraded riders along the water's edge.

Frankie heard voices from behind the Blue Lagoon. He decided against a getaway donkey and joined the Saturday crowd instead.

He tried to think.

He would have to deal with Barking's retribution at some point, but later was definitely a better option than sooner.

Speed, as he had confirmed with the careers adviser last week, was not his greatest asset, and ball control wasn't much help in a situation like this. He could cut up between the beach huts and lose himself in the alleys that threaded their way up the hill, but one wrong turn or a lucky guess on their part and he'd be in their hands. And anyway, if speed wasn't exactly his strongest suit, then speed *uphill* ranked even lower in his list of aptitudes.

That left trying to lose himself in the crowd. Even if they found him, they'd hardly be likely to start anything with people all about, would they?

He saw the gang emerge from behind the Blue Lagoon and then split up: Blunto and Arthur and a couple of others headed towards the pier, while Barking and Stu came this way. Frankie ducked his head down and walked as fast as he could.

A few minutes later, his clothes were soaked with sweat and he was gasping for breath.

He stopped and looked around.

He had reached where the cliffs started at the end of the beach huts, he realised. The crowds had thinned to a few families, one or two dog-walkers and not much else.

He sank to his haunches and hugged his knees.

He was shaking, and he was a little suspicious about the amount of wetness in his clothing. Big kids sweat a lot, but not usually that much.

Let them beat the crap out of him now, then, and get it over with.

That was when he heard the deep groaning again — almost a feeling rather than a sound, one that stole through your body and did things to your inner organs, your bones.

Furniture moving.

The sound set his teeth on edge, so that he just wanted the sensation to *stop*.

He'd had his eyes closed, but now he opened them and saw that things had changed. Back along the prom, the town had hunched its shoulders, and everything was taller, steeper, closer together, with buildings lined up at improbable angles and roads cutting up impossible slopes.

Fearful, he lowered his gaze.

Barking was pointing, Stu standing with his mouth open.

"How'd he cross the *creek*?" demanded Barking.

Stu shook his head, clearly unable to come up with an answer.

Frankie looked down. A deep creek full of churning white water cut between the two of them and where Frankie found himself now.

His pursuers stood at the end of the prom, where the ground tumbled away down the rocky banks of the creek.

Frankie himself was on a promontory, with a few scrubby bushes around him and the cliff rising to his left. He backed away.

He remembered the groaning of the earth, moments before.

His path hadn't crossed the creek. It was more the case that a new creek had crossed his path.

Home in his room, with the oil lamp turned down low, Frankie's head was buzzing with possibilities.

He lay back on his bed with his head nestled in his hands and his eyes closed. All the better to remember the looks of angered puzzlement on Stu and Barking's faces. They had been cheated of their victim and yet they didn't understand *how*.

He remembered the sense that the interior landscape of his daydreams had started to leak into the real world.

But perhaps it was the other way round.

Perhaps he had dragged the real world into the world of his dreams. Welcome to Faraway!

Whatever: Frankie had power here. He had shaped this world. And in his daydreams over the years he had re-shaped it and then re-shaped it again to suit his fantasies.

If he put his mind to it, he could have things exactly how he wanted.

He remembered Wookie's game: if you were ruler of the world what would you do? And Frankie's answer: he would change everything.

He got up and walked around his room. He was finding it hard to think.

Some time later, he realised that there was something nagging away at him. A doubt, a flaw.

The Owner.

Back in Nereby-on-Sea, the Owner was the one who was in control. But here... this was Frankie's world now. There was, as Frankie's fat counsellor would have said, an *issue* here. Eating for comfort had been an issue, as had encouraging people to laugh at his size because that meant they weren't looking too hard at the real Frankie. That's what she'd claimed. Large or medium fries had been more of an issue, as far as Frankie was concerned.

And now: the Owner. Someone should explain a few things to the Owner, Frankie thought. They needed to get a few ground rules straight.

But how would he do this? Could he just conjure up the Owner in the middle of his bedroom floor and explain a few things to him?

He even tried. For a few seconds, he sat on his bed with his eyes scrunched shut, thinking as hard as he could. But all he succeeded in doing was triggering a coughing fit as he realised thinking hard and holding his breath at the same time wasn't a good combination.

He went down to the first floor landing and found the phonebook on its shelf.

In his perfect world it would be as simple as... flicking through the telephone directory to the "O" section... running a finger down one column, then the next, until you reach "Ow"... and there:

Owner, The... Faraway

It didn't really say that, but for a moment the words flickered before Frankie's eyes, as if taunting him. There was nothing between "Owlsley, K" and "Owton, A".

He wasn't put off that easily, though. He would ask around. His father must know. Maybe someone at the school would know, or in the town hall, or the library.

He slept well that night, exhausted by his exertions and all the fresh air and sunshine. Despite the issue with Barking, he felt that there had been more positives than negatives today. A definite seven and a half out of ten.

That night, there were no further subterranean groans to disturb his sleep, no dreams that he could recall when he woke the next morning. Even the creaking of the Jolly Old Sea Captain pub sign didn't bother him now that he was in the attic room, on a higher level.

On Sunday morning he thought long and hard about starting the day with fifty sit-ups followed by the same number of press-ups. Just thinking about it brought him out in a light sweat, so he washed in the corner sink and dressed.

He looked out of the small leaded window. Since yesterday's upheavals, everything loomed closer, the houses leaning out over the street as if one day they would meet those on the other side. A morning mist was lifting, and the thin winter sunlight cast the street in an amber wash. The gas lamps had been put out and a horse and trap clattered by over the cobbles. A child in ragged clothing rummaged through a pile of black plastic bin liners, while a bony dog cocked its leg against some dark iron railings. On the other side, a nanny in a long grey coat and frilly bonnet pushed a pram the size of a small caravan. It was all very picturesque.

Frankie went down to the first-floor landing.

He saw that Grace's bedroom door was ajar, rather than firmly closed as it should be. He recalled Mother's behaviour of the previous day, and the cleared photographs and mementoes from the front room.

Had she been clearing up? Finally, after two years, moving on from their loss?

Surprised at how nervous he felt, Frankie stopped in the doorway and pushed the door gently open.

The room was gloomy, the heavy curtains drawn shut.

He could see the big old wardrobe covered with boy band posters, and a tall mirror with fairy lights strung around it.

He could see the linen basket, clothes still overflowing, and the upright pine bed with the duvet still turned down, as if his sister had only just got up. A half-full glass of water stood on the bedside cabinet, along with a stack of books and a notebook and pen.

Not a single thing had changed.

The smell of bacon drew him back out of his dead sister's room. He pulled the door ajar, and took a deep breath.

He missed Grace, so much.

His stomach rumbled.

He could deal with one of these things, at least, so he went downstairs.

In the kitchen, Mother was not alone.

A girl sat with her back to Frankie, tucking into a big breakfast. She had long dark hair that reminded him of the tangles of seaweed you would find along the foot of the pier at low tide. It was tied back with her favourite white ribbon this morning. And she wore the same slightly shabby red and white polka dot dress she had worn the day before.

Mother looked up, and smiled.

"Frankie," she said. "You great lazy lump. Your sister's up before you again."

Frankie stared.

Mother continued: "Grace, make some room for your brother at the table."

The girl looked up, grunted something through a mouthful of breakfast, and shuffled her chair along to make way.

6. An Improbable Return

Frankie sat.

Next to his sister.

Next to *Grace*.

He could hear her chewing. She always had chewed with her mouth open.

He could see her, out of the corner of his eye because he didn't dare look directly in case she vanished in a puff of smoke.

He could feel the occasional nudge of her elbow as she loaded up more food on her fork and raised it to her mouth.

Grace.

Finally, he looked at her.

She was older, of course. In the two years she had shed much of the puppy fat and become a young woman, no longer a spotty kid.

The eyes. He hadn't really seen her eyes yesterday. They were the same, though. Big and dark and round. Just like Frankie's eyes.

She glanced across and saw that he was staring. She cocked an eyebrow, an expression that ripped at his heart from across the years.

He felt... dizzy. He gripped the edge of the table. He sensed that deep, vibrating groan again, only this time it started deep inside: in his head, his heart, his bones. Things shifting, adjusting.

Of course it was Grace. Why hadn't he seen that yesterday? What foolishness had blinded him?

He remembered the two years since the accident: her time in hospital – was that a scar on her forehead? – the long hours he had spent with her, teaching her to walk again, teaching her to speak, teaching her about the world all over again.

She nodded towards something on the table, eyebrow still raised. "You pass the sauce please, Frannie?"

Only Grace had ever called him that, dating back to when they were little.

He took the ketchup bottle, offered it to her and clung on a split second too long, just so he could feel the resistance as she tugged it from his grip.

She was real.

She squeezed the bottle and it belched sauce over her bacon. "Thanks, Frannie," she said, absent-mindedly. He saw the silver bracelet dangling on her slim wrist as she tipped the bottle.

Frankie looked down. His mother had put a plate before him. He poked at a mushroom with a fork. He wasn't hungry, but he cleared his plate anyway.

"Where's Father?" he asked.

Mother paused, her hands deep in dirty dishwater.

"He went out early," she said. "He says the crowds are going to be good again today. Doesn't want to miss out. He's obsessed by that place. Doesn't want to disappoint the Owner, he says."

Frankie was reminded of his thoughts the previous evening. Things shouldn't be like this in Faraway. Father should be happy too.

"Don't worry," he said. "I'm sure everything will sort itself out."

The two of them went down streets so steep they had to walk sideways and cling to the iron lamp posts as they went. They bought huge gobstoppers from a machine outside a shop that had not been there the day before. They cut down an alleyway where Frankie actually had to turn his shoulders to squeeze between the buildings, while Grace just ducked low and ran.

Clear of the alley, Frankie ran after her and caught up easily, which meant she must have been giving him a chance. She laughed an infectious laugh, and they slowed, and walked on down to where the path joined the prom by Buckets And Spades.

They went inside for ice creams. Frankie had a Magnum. Grace had a Strawberry Mivi. They came outside and stood by the railing.

The crowd wasn't as big today as on Saturday, but then it was earlier. The tide was low, so that children had to paddle through mud to reach the water. The donkeys lined up in the shade of a stripy canopy, each wearing straw hat, blinkers and a nose bag.

The stalls along the prom were open already, and barrel organ music drifted towards the two of them from further along.

"BPP?" asked Grace. "Beach, prom or pier? It's your turn to decide."

He didn't argue. He couldn't remember whose turn it must be. "Beach," he said. He wanted to talk to Father, but that could wait: he didn't want to take Grace to the pier just for that. And the prom hadn't worked out too well yesterday. The beach was an altogether better option.

They took the metal steps down to the beach and headed across the loose sand and stones to the high tide mark, where the ground was firmer. Dried seaweed formed a line here, littered with driftwood, sea-smoothed glass bottles, a couple of old shoes. The wet sand was easier walking, as long as you paid enough attention to sidestep the elaborate, teetering sandcastle constructions that had gone up this morning and now awaited the advance of the tide.

They headed for the footings of the pier, exposed by the low tide. It was dark here. Great tarred timbers, as thick as... well... as big trees, rose from the sand and mud to support the weight of the pier. Cross beams connected the uprights, held in place by bolts the size of Frankie's arm, and a network of iron rods criss-crossed through it all, binding the supports in a spider's web cradle.

Frankie stood and peered directly above his head. Look down through the gaps between the boards on the pier and you saw the sea. But looking up, he saw heavy planks, and beams and rods – no sign of the lights of the amusements, or of the bottoms of people's feet as they stood at gaming machines or wandered from attraction to attraction.

"Look!"

Grace was a short distance away, squatting down, pointing into a pool.

Frankie went to join her. An anemone the size of his fist was just below the surface of the water. It was fully open, hundreds of tentacles swirling and grasping in the water – yellow tentacles, orange ones, a few shading into a livid red.

"Isn't it beautiful?" She tipped back onto her heels and looked all around them. "Isn't it *all* beautiful, Frannie?"

He looked. The timbers were clotted with old tar, cracking and tangled with seaweed. Rubbish had blown in and trapped itself around the woodwork. Beyond, the beach formed a sharp, pale yellow strip, slowly filling up with families, couples, old folk in their laid-right-back stripy deckchairs. The prom, only glimpsed from here, was lined with stalls and shops and, further along, gaudy beach huts, the town bunched up on the slope behind.

He looked back at Grace and nodded. "It's not bad," he said. "Not bad at all, when you take everything into account."

She started to wander on, and he trailed after her. "I saw you yesterday," he said.

She rolled her eyes at him. "Course you did, Frannie."

He persisted. "At the Punch and Judy show."

She looked puzzled.

"You ran off."

Understanding dawned. "The clay man," she said. "His head broke. Didn't you think that was unbearably sad, Frannie? Have you got no soul?"

"I've got three," he said. He raised a foot and pointed. "My left sole, my right sole, and my ar…"

She flicked a bunch of seaweed at him and darted off between the pier's support timbers. He ran after her.

This time she wasn't giving any chances, and she hared away across the beach, long legs flying high, sand kicking up in her wake.

He ran for a time. Further than he could remember running before. Even at school, the cross-country run for him was far more of a gentle jog and then a long, long walk, with Mr Witsend urging him along so he wouldn't be late for his next lesson.

He lost her, and a sudden rush of panic engulfed him, the fear of losing her all over again.

He walked on. A couple of gulls took off from the beach before him, then landed a short distance further on, only to repeat the process when he caught up with them again.

The beach was deserted, cliffs rising up to his left, the sea creeping in from the right. It seemed that this no-man's land would go on for ever.

"Oi, dreamer!"

She was up the beach. She'd been lying down, but now she sat up and he saw her head and shoulders over the ridged-up high-tide mark. He climbed the beach to join her, then flopped down in the loose sand at her side.

The sun beat down out of a perfect blue sky.

"Caught you," he said. They had spent so many long summer days like this. They weren't just twins, they were best friends.

"You cool, little brother?"

"I'm cool." Nine minutes difference in their ages, that was all.

"You're looking good, Frannie."

He looked down at himself. He could see his feet, his knees, and not just because his bulk had settled around him as he lay down. He was still big-built but... he sensed that something had shifted again.

"Hmm," he said. He felt good, too: about life, about himself, about Grace. "You're not too bad yourself, sis'."

He thought then of Wookie's Ruler of the World game. He

rolled onto his side, propping himself up on an elbow.

Grace lay back, arms stretched above her head, eyes shut. She was hardly moving at all, and for a moment Frankie felt that rush of panic again. Then she took a shallow, almost imperceptible, breath, and he relaxed.

"Grace," he said. She opened her eyes, as if sensing his seriousness. "If you could change anything – anything at all – about this world, what would it be?"

He would do it. Whatever she asked. He would dream it and dream it until her wish just had to come true.

She smirked. "Change anything?" she said. "Why nothing at all, Frannie. Why would I want to change anything? Everything's perfect just as it is."

Back at home that evening, they ate pan-fried chicken and pilau rice that Mother had managed not to reduce to mush, and they told her about their day, and she listened.

Father was still out at work. "But that must be good," Mother assured them.

They put on a Laurel and Hardy DVD and laughed uproariously when Ollie kept getting hit by a plank of wood and Stan kept happening to duck at just the right moment.

When Father came in, he looked tired but satisfied.

"How's the One-armed Bandit?" Frankie asked him, as his father sank into a deep armchair, a bottle of beer in one hand and the newspaper in the other.

"Hmm? Oh, yes. He's tired, Frankie. Very tired. People keep coming in and pulling his arm."

"That's good," said Frankie.

Father nodded. "Yes, son, I suppose it is."

Frankie and Grace retreated upstairs. Frankie sat on the windowsill, peering out at the advancing night fog as it muffled the gas lamps down to feeble sparks of light.

Grace sat on her bed, her back against the wall and her knees drawn up to her chin.

They sat in companionable silence for a time.

Frankie wondered what was in his sister's head. He'd always felt this about her: everyone was the centre of their own universe; his sister was as close to him as anyone and yet... the inside of her head was a foreign land, a distant planet, an entire separate universe.

"Why have I still got those up, I wonder?" she said, nodding towards the boy band posters on her wardrobe, at least a couple of years out of date.

"Bad taste is the most likely explanation," Frankie told her. He'd always hated these posters. "Shall I take them down?"

"Yes, Frannie, do. I don't like them anymore."

He went across and started to un-stick them.

"And this?" she said. She was holding the conch shell up towards Frankie. "Why have I got this?"

"You always loved that," said Frankie. Perhaps everything wasn't quite perfect yet, he thought. But it would be, he felt sure. "You put it to your ear so you can hear the sea."

"Yeah, right," she said. "You're pulling my leg, Frannie."

"Not really the sea, of course," said Frankie. "It's the blood pulsing in your ear: it echoes in the shell and sounds like waves crashing on the beach. You always believed it was true before, though."

She shrugged, and raised the shell to her ear. She frowned. "I can't hear a thing," she said after a while.

"Keep trying, Grace," he said. "You'll hear it."

Finally, her eyes sparkled, and a sudden smile tugged at her mouth. She looked at him. "I can hear it," she whispered. "I really can."

He returned to de-boybanding the wardrobe.

"It's been a good day, hasn't it, Frannie?"

He nodded. "Nine out of ten, I reckon," he said. A clear nine. They don't come much better.

Later that night, when his mother was in the bathroom, Frankie slipped downstairs again. His father was sitting in an armchair in the corner of the dining room with the folded newspaper on his lap.

"Good weekend, Father? The town seems busy for the time of year." Frankie sat at the table.

"Fair to middling," said Father. "Not bad for the off-season."

"The Owner must be pleased with the takings."

His father waggled his head from side to side. So so.

"I reckon he must have a huge house," said Frankie. "A mansion. One of those big places up on the cliffs, with a view out across the bay. So he can sit in an overstuffed armchair by the window and survey all that he owns."

"Wouldn't surprise me," said Father. "Probably has one of them big town houses back of the prom, too, for when he can't be bothered to go all the way home to the prime clifftop residence at night. Wouldn't be surprised at all. Probably got a chateau in the south of France, as well, for those self-indulgent summer breaks."

"So what's he like then?" asked Frankie.

"Don't deal with him myself, these days," said Father. "I'm not that high up the pecking order, me. I only ever deal with his people, his representatives. They take the cash box at the end of the day, and they pay my wages at the end of the week, and that's good enough for me. It keeps us in biscuits, doesn't it?"

Frankie thought back to the evening when he'd hidden behind the cut-out muscle man and seen – or rather heard – Father handing over the arcade's takings to the Owner's representative.

"So…"

He stopped. His father's head had tipped back, his mouth open so that his little crooked teeth showed. He was fast asleep.

Frankie went back up to bed.

In the morning, they all ate breakfast together, and then the proud parents watched as Frankie and Grace set off up the hill to school.

Frankie and his sister had identical brown leather satchels slung over their shoulders, with doorstop sandwiches wrapped in greaseproof paper tucked away inside. The street was steep this morning, but Frankie didn't mind the extra effort.

"This way," he said, leading Grace round the sharp bend towards the junction with Smugglers' Row.

Grace looked pale today. Nervous. She never had liked school. She was a child who ran barefoot along wide open beaches, not one who found it easy to follow timetables and rules and write exactly what you had to in order to pass an exam instead of the poem that had just popped into your head and needed writing down *now*. School wasn't made for people like Grace.

"No!" He called after her. "You don't want to go along there. You want to go up here."

She stopped and turned. Frankie pointed up the path. They had reached the Drop.

She came back and tipped her head to look up the hill. "Up there?" she said, uncertainly. "Yeah, right."

Frankie looked. The path was steep, bulging in places so that it was almost vertical. But this was The Route To School. He always came this way.

"This is the way," he told her. "We always come this way, don't we?"

She peered up the path again. After a couple of seconds she said, "Yes. Yes, we always come this way, Frannie. Come on: I'll race you!"

She grabbed the iron rail attached to the side of one of the houses and hauled herself up.

Frankie followed, digging the toes of his boots into the cracks between the big cobbles and pulling on the railing.

She maintained her lead, just as she always did. They passed back-to-back backyards, and another row of houses, then crossed a street before the slope kicked in again. Past the next line of backyards, the Drop cut through a craggy headland, and then opened out into an area with a couple of benches and an overflowing litter bin.

They paused for breath.

"What a view," gasped Grace.

Frankie looked. A beam of sunlight cut through heavy grey clouds, lighting the town in a golden spotlight. Rooftops tumbled away below them, lines of them criss-crossing at unnatural angles, the tiles scabbed yellow and orange with lichen and great big clumps of moss. It was like this all the way down to the sea, the last line of rooftops cutting into the bay like teeth. The bay itself was a deep slate grey, taking its colour from the storm clouds and from its silty depths, and the pier stretched out into the distance.

It was just how he'd always imagined.

They came to the cornershop, with its bullseye glass in the windows and displays of vegetables outside so fresh that there was dirt from the fields on them.

Frankie swung in through the door.

"Good morning."

He'd forgotten about mechanical not-Cindy behind the counter. He stopped and looked at her. She was still the same: the china doll red circle on each cheek, the unnatural stillness and the jerky mechanical movements. Quite efficient, he supposed. Not a bad way to run a shop.

He gathered up a Mars and a packet of ready salted and reached for his change.

"That will be... eight-y... sev-en... pence, please." She put a hand out palm-up for his money.

He gave her a fifty and two twenties.

"Thank you. You have tendered... nine-ty... pence... only."

He waited for his change – "Your change is... three pence" – and then turned.

Grace had come no further than the doorway. "You cool?" he asked her.

She looked past him at not-Cindy and gave a tiny shake of her head. She looked as if Mr Punch had shattered his head all over again.

He followed after her, but she walked head down, not responding to anything he said.

They joined the flow of pupils heading into school past the arts and technology block, an ugly grey concrete building with long windows and scrubbed clean patches where they'd removed the graffiti.

Rounding the corner, they came into view of the main building: tall, with red brick walls and high metal-framed windows. The punishment cage was suspended high from the flagpole, empty, its door swinging open in the breeze.

Grace had stopped.

"It's okay," said Frankie. "It's only there for the worst offenders."

She nodded, and caught up with him.

They went into the building, jostling and pushing in the corridor. When they reached their form class, they went to their desk in the middle of the room, where they always sat side by side for registration. It was an old desk, polished by generations of elbows resting, bored. Frankie opened the lid, put his satchel inside and sat back.

Slowly, the class filled up.

Wookie came in and sat at the next desk. "Dude," he said and

Frankie nodded in return. "Dude-ess," Wookie added, leaning past Frankie to address Grace.

She smiled, still nervous.

Barking came in then, trailing Stu and Blunto and Marji behind him just as he trailed his school bag on the floor. He eyed Frankie straight away, then ran a finger across his neck, signalling Frankie's ultimate fate.

Frankie had expected as much. He would have been disappointed with anything less from young Harry Barker. He smiled and gave a little finger-twiddling wave as Barker led his posse through to the row behind Frankie and Grace.

"You're dead, Finnegan," Barking hissed, just in case Frankie had misinterpreted his throat-slitting gesture.

Frankie placed a finger on his wrist, as if to take his own pulse. After a few seconds he shook his head. Barking was clearly wrong about his state of being.

If you're going to dig a hole, Frankie Finnegan always believed in digging it as deep as possible.

But by his side, Grace reached across and briefly put a hand on his arm. "Don't," she muttered.

He could feel her trembling. School really didn't suit her. Or maybe it was Barking and his gang who were frightening her.

Things hadn't always been like this. Once upon a time, well, they hadn't exactly been best of friends but at least Barking had tolerated Frankie's presence when he and Grace had been part of the group. The boy had been okay before he had started taking things out on Frankie.

But now...

"Your sister's a bit whiffy today, Finnegan," said Barker. "Shouldn't she have her annual bath around now?"

Marji sniggered.

Frankie hadn't noticed until now, but he had to admit that Grace did have a certain aroma about her. Salty, like old seaweed or mud newly uncovered by the tide. Not an unpleasant smell, just different.

He turned. "Kindly desist, Mr Barker," he said. "You're a cad and a bounder and it's just not fair."

Barking stared at him. Finally, he shook his head. First round to Frankie.

Mr Cray came in then, wearing the same frock coat and mutton chop whiskers he had on Friday. The class fell silent as he surveyed them, then he nodded and seated himself.

Frankie leaned across to Grace and whispered, "It's okay, Grace. It's always safe to ignore rude comments when they come from single-celled organisms."

A sharp crack like a gunshot echoed around the room.

Mr Cray had rapped an ink jar down on his desk, and now he was staring at Frankie.

Frankie straightened, smiling at Mr Cray.

Their teacher started to work through the register.

"Daly, S?"

"Sir."

"Evans, D?"

"Sir."

"Finnegan, F?"

No interruption today, no dull repetition of the same old joke. "Present, Mr Cray, sir," he said.

"Finnegan, G?"

"Stinks," hissed a voice.

"Needs a wash," whispered another.

"Puke-face," another.

"Finnegan, G?" A glare, right at Grace.

"Sir," she said in a wavering voice. "Present, sir."

"Harvey, I?" And on.

They rounded on Frankie and Grace at lunchtime. Up against the wall of the science block, Frankie clutched his satchel to his chest; by his side, Grace did exactly the same with hers.

"You Finnegans," sneered Barking. "You're disgusting, in't

you? You're pond-life."

Frankie considered the merits of pointing out to his tormentor that Frankie had used a very similar insult to Barking only that morning, so repeating it to him so soon wasn't particularly smart. He decided against this.

Barking strode around in front of the two of them, while Stu, Blunto and three others lined up at his shoulder.

"But this one..." he nodded towards Grace. "Look at her! Filthy, stinking, ugly. Shouldn't be allowed out."

Frankie glanced at his sister and for a moment saw her as she was. She was a wild thing, a primitive, like a startled deer or a swallow cutting through summer skies. She didn't belong here. She belonged on the beach, or on long walks across the clifftops. Someone like Grace should never be tied down by school...

She was easy prey for the likes of Harry Barker, that was for sure.

Frankie weighed up his options.

He could try to talk his way out of this. He'd managed that before with Barking, who it had to be said wasn't exactly the sharpest toothpick in the pack. But they were backed up against a wall, and rather heavily outnumbered.

Or he could just take the initiative, knee Barking in the nuts and hope that he and Grace could extract themselves in the ensuing chaos.

None of the options looked promising, but the thought of doing Barking some damage had its attractions.

Mr Cray saved him from having to make a decision. He strode right into the middle of the group and demanded, "What's going on here? Barker? Finnegan? An explanation."

"We's just talking," muttered Barking, staring at the ground.

"You's just earned youself an infringement for improper use of the Queen's English," said Mr Cray. "Finnegan?"

Frankie smiled. "As Barker said, we were just passing the time of day," he told their teacher. "Despite appearances, Barker and I get along famously, don't we, Harold?"

Barking glowered at him.

Frankie leaned towards Mr Cray, and added, "But I feel it is my duty, Mr Cray, sir, to remind you that *you haven't punished Barker yet.*"

Mr Cray looked at him, a puzzled expression on his face. He put a hand to the side of his head. Frankie knew what he was feeling: the groaning, deep within, the shifting, the re-adjusting...

Mr Cray shuddered and straightened. "Barker," he said. "Come with me."

Barking stared in disbelief, but he had no choice and he trotted along at the master's heels, heading back into the main building.

Stu and Blunto and the others dissolved away into the lunchtime crowd immediately. They didn't want to have anything to do with Frankie.

So Frankie turned to his sister and smiled. "Where were we?" he asked, as if they had just been distracted in mid-conversation.

But Grace was watching as Barking and Mr Cray disappeared into the building.

When they had gone, she turned her big dark eyes on Frankie. "That was unnecessary," she told him. "Behaving like that makes you just like them."

She walked past him, and he stared at the space she had occupied. Then when he turned she had gone altogether.

She sat next to him in class for the rest of the afternoon, as Mr Cray drilled them in Latin and trigonometry and sandstorm physics. But she didn't speak to him, and she barely even glanced in his direction.

She could get like this sometimes. He had forgotten. Just as he had forgotten the little tic in the corner of her left eye when she was angry, and the way she could point out things he had overlooked and make them seem completely obvious. Like two and two *do* equal four, and an eye for an eye is really rather silly and childish when you think about it.

He chose not to think about any of this. Barker had it coming. And thinking of Barker... he wasn't in class now: Mr Cray must have sent him somewhere else for what remained of the day.

When they left school at the end of the afternoon, a small crowd had gathered on the main playground. They were pointing, yelling names and insults, all looking up at the front of the main building.

The cage.

It was suspended about three-quarters of the way up the flagpole, swaying a little from side to side, the pole bending under the strain.

A figure, tiny at this distance, sat in a corner of the cage, tipping it to one side, one leg stretched out, the other bent.

Barking, serving out his punishment.

Frankie walked home alone. Grace had gone on ahead.

She was waiting for him on the open area halfway down the Drop. She sat on one of the benches, swinging her legs, tipping her head back to catch the afternoon sunshine.

She was a different person again: the Grace who ran barefoot on the beach, not the cooped up animal of school.

"Hey," he said, sitting on the far end of the bench. "Good day at school?"

"Like a dodo," she said. Over, dead, extinct: she didn't want to talk about it.

Frankie felt the sun on his face. It felt good, like Grace's forgiveness.

He felt that way about school, too.

Over, dead, extinct.

Dodo.

8. Things To Do After School

The evening was a little cooler but even so they went down to the prom. The bay was calm again, and a low mist clung to its surface.

It was extraordinarily peaceful.

Frankie and Grace stood at the railing by Buckets And Spades and looked out over the bay for a long, long time.

They walked, stepping aside for a young couple exercising a lollipop miniature poodle, the man in stripy blazer and a straw boater, the woman clinging to his arm in frills and bustle and a tight corset that pinched her waist like a wasp's.

They stopped and watched an old man cranking a barrel organ, while a tiny, wiry monkey chained to the organ by its collar danced an off-beat jig.

They came to a conjuror in bow tie and stovepipe hat, and watched him produce a succession of white doves from his handkerchief pocket. They stayed as he fashioned modelling clay into the shape of a small rabbit and then with a wave of the hand... it was a white rabbit, nose twitching, ears flopping. When he started on card tricks, they moved on.

"Do you think summer could last forever?" Frankie asked his sister.

This wasn't quite summer, though. But it certainly wasn't winter. More like a fine day in early May, the kind of day that holds out the promise of better things to come.

"Why not?" said Grace.

It wasn't summer for everyone, though.

They came near to the pier and stopped again. Leaning on the rails, Frankie saw a young woman down on the beach, a bundle of something at her bare feet.

At first, Frankie thought little of the sight. Just someone out enjoying what remained of the afternoon sun.

Then he recognised the dark, standing-up hair and the way she held herself. Cindy.

He hadn't seen Cindy for days. He had barely even given her a thought. The cornershop still did what it was meant to do, just as efficiently as before, so why should she come into his thoughts?

The bundle at her feet: something wrapped up in blankets. Her possessions, he realised. With a flash of clarity he knew that what he saw was her life in its entirety: all she had, there on the beach at her feet.

He went down the steps and crunched over the sand and shingle towards her.

"Hey, Cindy," he said. "How's things?"

She looked up and smiled. "Hi, Frankie," she said. "Good day at school? Hi there, Grace." Cindy looked much younger now, without her make-up. She could only be a couple of years older than Frankie and Grace.

"Sure," said Frankie. "Are you okay? I haven't seen you for a while."

She smiled. "Nice of you to ask, Frankie. I'm not so bad, considering I lost my job and all."

"We were just going to get some chips. Do you fancy some?"

She shrugged, but Frankie went up to Fast Fries anyway and bought some from mechanical Mr Singh. When he came back down, Frankie spread the paper on the beach between the three of them, but he and Grace barely touched the chips while Cindy wolfed them down.

Afterwards, they sat together until the sun had gone, and then Frankie and Grace returned up the steep streets of Faraway to their home, leaving Cindy with her small bundle of possessions on the beach.

Grace was even more nervous in the morning than she had been the previous day. School again, and it was only Tuesday. Four whole days to go until the weekend.

It really should be summer every day, thought Frankie. Summer holidays every day of the week.

"You cool?" he said to her, as he sat down for breakfast.

She smiled, then looked away. A caged animal.

He wondered if she had heard the shiftings in the night, the subterranean groans. They had woken Frankie from a dream, and he had lain awake, heart pounding, caught between two realities. The earth had sounded like an injured animal to him, then.

Up to Rigormortis Road and then clambering, hauling their way up the Drop, they made their way to school. Frankie tried to make conversation – the conjuror, the dancing monkey, Cindy – but there was no getting through to Grace today.

When they came to the cornershop Frankie peered in through the bullseye windows.

He could tell that Grace didn't want to go in, and now he thought again of Cindy on the beach with her pathetic bundle. They walked past.

They passed through the lower school gates, by art and technology, just as they always did, just two among a steady flow of blue-blazered pupils.

They rounded the corner.

And stopped.

Kids stood around in small groups, or alone. They talked and pointed and nudged. They all looked in the same direction, towards the main school building.

The school was in ruins.

In places the roof had collapsed, in others it sagged or there were tiles missing. There was no glass in the windows. Doors hung off their hinges, and the walls of the media lab extension had collapsed. Ivy grew over it all, and giant crows perched on exposed timbers, surveying their territory.

It looked like a building that had been abandoned decades ago, a hundred years, perhaps.

"No school today then," said Frankie. "What a shame."

School was like a dodo.

Over, dead, extinct.

He looked at Grace, expecting to see relief flooding her features, but instead she looked shocked. "What have you done?" she whispered, and then plunged through the crowd.

He followed, perplexed by her response. She *hated* school. Couldn't stand the place.

She stopped and waited for him, then pointed. "You have to get him down, Frannie."

The cage! He looked up. Barking was still up there, lying in the cage, curled up like a sleeping baby.

He had been there all night.

They came to the foot of the flagpole and found where the rope had been secured. There was a bolt and a handle that controlled some kind of pulley. He took hold of the handle, released the bolt, and then began to turn.

Slowly, creaking, the cage lowered.

When it hit the ground, Barking reached through the bars and released the door. He stepped out and brushed himself down.

"Why not thank me, Barking?" demanded Frankie. "It could have been far, far worse."

Barking stared at him, then turned slowly and walked off through the crowd.

"Next time," Frankie called after him. Then more quietly, he added, "Just you wait until next time..."

He turned. A group had gathered by what remained of the media lab. They shouted and cheered as they hauled on a piece of wood protruding from the ruins. After a short time, the wood came clear and the members of the group staggered, as another section of wall slumped to the ground.

They all laughed and slapped each other on the backs, and

Frankie laughed too.

A yell went up from what had once – very long time ago – been the main entrance to the school. Izzy Harvey had emerged, with the school flag wrapped around his waist like a sari, and now other pupils were poking and tugging at it.

Frankie nodded in approval.

This was his world.

These were his rules.

The old order had crumbled before him.

But Grace...

She had stayed back in the middle of the playground when he came to get Barking down. Now she watched Frankie warily.

He went to her.

"You never did like school, did you?" he said.

"What have you done, Frankie?" she asked once again. "Why must you upset everything?"

"But you hated all this!"

"And so *this* is an improvement?"

Over by the gym, Mr Witsend had emerged and was now being chased by a group of children who swung their bags at him and whooped like Apaches.

Frankie shrugged. Things certainly didn't seem any worse to him.

"I did this for you," he said. "I couldn't stand the thought of you having to get through another day like yesterday. The bullying, the taunts... the double maths."

She smiled, briefly. "Oh, Frannie," she said. Then, serious again: "But can't you see that this makes you just as bad as all the others?"

He gritted his teeth.

He wasn't like the others! He didn't find someone's weak spot and pick at it over and over and over like the drip drip dripping of a tap. He didn't tell lies about people and trick them into getting into trouble. He didn't carefully cultivate everyone else so that they were either on their own or part of the mob, and then turn that mob on the few who stood out.

He *was* different.

His eyes stung.

He blinked, and then looked away.

When he looked back, Mr Witsend had gone down under the mob and Grace had gone altogether.

The Owner's enforcers cornered him in an alleyway between High Street and the promenade.

He was at a loose end, roaming, not really understanding the mixture of feelings competing within. Triumph that school was so well and truly over. But also, dismay at Grace's response. She didn't seem to understand that this world could be exactly how they wanted it. In Faraway it really could be summer forever.

He had gone past the fishmonger's shop, with its tank of crabs climbing over each other in the window.

He didn't know where Grace had gone, and he wasn't sure if he wanted to find her just yet, in any case. He didn't want her being cross with him still. And he didn't want her being all sunny and forgiving while he still sorted things out in his head.

He had turned into one of the many passages that led between High Street and prom. There were people ahead. Four of them. Two leaned against the wall, and two stood with hands in jacket pockets.

One of them was Harry Barker.

Frankie glanced over his shoulder, and considered turning on his heel. But he'd dealt with Barking already. There shouldn't be any more trouble there for a while.

He kept going.

Two of them, both tall and thin men, stepped back jerkily to allow Frankie through, then the third man stepped in his way. Just as Frankie recognised this man, he realised he had been trapped, with the two others now blocking his retreat.

Before him stood Barking and the young man with the cold grey eyes who had come to collect the arcade cash-box from Father. The Owner's representative.

The two of them side by side could have been brothers, the one in his too-big suit, the other in school blazer and tie. Both had thin faces with sharp nose and chin, and chilly grey eyes. Both carried themselves like fighters.

"So, Francis Finnegan." The rep spoke as if he was reading from a cue card. "Francis, son of Michael, proprietor of Pier Amusements and Entertainments."

If Barking hadn't been there, Frankie would have considered for more than the merest split second the feasibility of claiming mistaken identity. "At your service," he said, instead.

"I hear school's out," said the rep. "Barking here told me all about what happened."

Frankie nodded.

"So you can consider this a part of your continuing education," said the man. "Extra-curricular." He smirked, and Barking smirked right back at him.

Frankie looked towards the high street and for the first time realised that the other two members of this mob were mechanicals, like not-Cindy and Mr Singh in Fast Fries. They stood motionless, like shop-window mannequins, their eyes fixed on him. They had pale china skin, with pink patches on each cheek and eyebrows painted on. Whoever made them hadn't bothered to do a good job: they were merely adequate, functional constructions.

"My education..." said Frankie, returning his attention to the Owner's representative.

"That's right, Finnegan. Education. You see, it might come as something of a surprise to you, but this is not your world, and it's not your town. We already have an owner, and up to now everything's been ticking over real smooth."

He pulled a hand from his jacket pocket and a blade flashed.

He had a flick-knife. He proceeded to pick at his fingernails with it. "Like I say," he continued, "we've noticed a few... *upheavals*... lately, and my good friend Barking tells me that you're at the centre of it. He thinks we should just slice you right now –"

Those eyes: they fixed on Frankie like headlights.

"– but I don't think we need to be that drastic, do we, Finnegan? Because you're not going to do anything stupid again, are you? You're going to leave things exactly as they are."

Frankie's throat was dry. He tried to swallow. Tried to speak. In the end he merely nodded.

They left him, one of the mechanicals brushing past him as they marched out of the alleyway. So close, he could hear the whirr and clunk of their inner mechanisms.

That evening, he sat on the windowsill in Grace's room, watching rats skitter about in the roadway while children played with hoops and sticks nearby.

Grace appeared to have forgiven him, which didn't make things much better, as he wasn't quite sure what it was that had required forgiving.

"Will you help me?" he said, into one of their long silences.

She cocked an eyebrow, waiting for him to explain.

"I need to find the Owner," he said. "I need to stop him pushing people around." That's *my* job. This is *my* world.

She stayed silent.

"I was there a few days ago when one of his men was pushing Father around. And... today they tried it with me. Told me to stop trying to influence things."

"Maybe they were right," said Grace. "Maybe you shouldn't rock the boat."

She sounded like they had. He'd hoped for something more.

"Look at what we've got, Frannie! You don't need to change anything."

"But... how can I control what I want? This is my world,

Grace. This is Faraway! This is where we've always escaped to. All those stories we used to make up, all the games we played. We're here now, Grace. Faraway seems to have come out of my head somehow. This isn't something I planned, it just *is*."

"Well whatever this is," said Grace. "You have to take responsibility. You can't risk blowing everything away. You should just leave things as they are now. For us: for the family. Don't go causing trouble. And don't go turning your back on us, either. You can't abandon us now: if this is Faraway, then where else can you escape to? You have to make a go of things here."

She was telling him he was trapped: trapped in his own imagination.

"Don't blow it, Frannie. D'you hear?"

He looked at her. Grace. His sister.

"I don't want to go back there again," she said quietly. "I'll do anything not to have to go away again."

9. A Case Of Replacement (part one)

That night, Frankie had his nightmare about the Jolly Old Sea Captain again. It was a long time since he'd had this particular dream.

He dreamed that he was lying awake in his bed, his room flooded with silvery moonlight. The pub sign was creaking, even though there was no breeze to move it. He climbed from his bed, momentarily terrified even to put his bare feet on the floor.

From his window, he peered down. The pub sign was moving, as if rocked by an unseen hand, and it was blank. The old sea captain had gone roaming.

Fears can be so intense when you're dreaming. Frankie sat on his windowsill, surveying the street, alert to even the slightest sound coming from within the house. Nothing stirred the night fog, and the gas streetlamps cast no unexpected shadows.

The stairs creaked.

He knew this was only the sound of a house at night, its timbers expanding or contracting as they cooled.

A shadow! Out in the fog, a dark shape where the gas-lamp's beam was interrupted. A man, shambling along, like one of the Owner's automatons, his arms held out before him like Boris Karloff as Frankenstein's monster. The figure wore a brass-buttoned navy blue blazer, and a white seaman's cap was perched on his head. Grey whiskers extended down the sides of his face and there would almost certainly be a pipe dangling from the corner of his mouth and a ruddy glow to his cheeks.

The Jolly Old Sea Captain...

The figure stopped, and looked directly at Frankie.

The Jolly Old Sea Captain looked just like Mr Cray!

Frankie drew back into the shadows. Seconds later, the old sea captain had gone.

And then he heard another creak of timbers coming from within the house – the stairs, or the first floor landing.

And another.

Another.

He lay there, wide awake, and realised that he was no longer asleep, no longer dreaming, and the house was in silence.

He got up and padded across to the small leaded window. The scene was almost exactly as he had dreamed: the fog, the feeble gas light combined with silvery moonlight. But there was no Jolly Old Sea Captain in the street and when Frankie craned to see, the pub sign was not blank.

He went back to bed, and concentrated on pleasant thoughts.

Frankie and Grace built sandcastles and waited for the tide to come in.

Frankie had filled buckets and inverted them, then chipped away at the moist sand to reveal walls and crenellations. He dug a deep moat around his best castle, and then built a sand causeway across it to the west gate, which he had protected with a portcullis made from lolly sticks. Then he dug a channel down the beach in order to divert seawater into the moat as the tide advanced. As a finishing touch, he made tiny clay figures and set them around the castle's defences.

Grace had stared at the flat sand for an eternity, as if she was trying to see something, or sense it. And then, on her knees, she leaned forward and started to scoop sand into a giant mound. A hill took shape, and it looked like a hill that had always been there, a hill that *should* be there. Working with incredible precision, she then began to craft walls, roofs and terraces so meticulously that you could easily imagine hundreds of tiny people living within.

"But how do you defend it?" Frankie asked.

She waggled her head from side to side. "I don't," she told him. "It just *is*. This is how it should be and so I'm not trying to control everything and interfere."

Frankie felt under attack, but wasn't quite sure how she had managed to turn a simple, childish activity into a moral.

"But it's a castle," he said. "Sand-*castle*. That's what it is."

He had to acknowledge, though, that hers was pretty neat.

When the tide crept in, Frankie's battlements crumbled, undermined by the water in his moat. His clay figures fell, dissolving in the water. Soon his castle was little more than a sludgy hummock, while somehow the water flowed around Grace's so that her sand hill village stood for a long time above the waves before finally succumbing.

Returning down to the beach from Fast Fries with lunch, they said hello to Cindy again. She had a bunch of ragamuffin kids with her today. They were dressed in filthy, tattered school uniforms and had sooty smudges on their faces but they seemed cheerful enough.

Frankie and Grace sat with them and shared their chips around. They had bought plenty.

Frankie noticed that most of the day-trippers and holidaymakers gave this group a wide berth, as if they knew the kids didn't belong. He saw the girl who had been in detention with him and Barking last week – Thingummy Cochrane. He nodded at her, and she smiled back.

"How's things?" Frankie asked.

"Not so bad," said Cindy. "We don't have much to live on and we don't have proper homes, but we're making do. I don't really understand what's happening to the world any more. It's beyond me."

She hugged herself.

"But hey, things could be worse, couldn't they?" She gestured towards her ragamuffin band. "They're a great bunch of kids. The school's closed down, so they don't have any reason to be here anymore. None of us have any roles in this place. So we sit on the beach and get by."

He hadn't thought about what must happen to people in Faraway when they no longer had a reason to exist. If there was no school then there was no need for pupils and teachers. All these bit-part players in his daydream world – they were superfluous.

Cindy smiled. "We need to sort ourselves out, though. We need to stay active and find some kind of a role, or the Owner will tidy us all away. So I'm teaching them stuff. I taught a couple of them to pick pockets, and some of the others find change on the beach or mind deck-chairs while Old Archie has a smoke. We're doing all right, we are."

"Where do you live?" Frankie asked. "Where do you sleep?"

"Oh, in between places," said Cindy. "There are lots of gaps where we can slot ourselves away. You thinking of joining us?"

He shook his head. He had a home, he had his family. He had everything he wanted.

He had to confront the Owner, even though Grace didn't want him to interfere. She wanted him to keep things exactly as they were: they both had everything they wanted.

But Father still worked all hours, and when he was home he just slept, exhausted. He was driven by his need to keep the Owner's representative happy with the heft of his cashbox. And there were Cindy and the schoolkids, too, believing they had to justify their existence or be wiped away.

This was Faraway, a world sprung from Frankie's head. The Owner had no right to control things in this way.

Late that afternoon, Frankie was alone, out on the pier.

He paid his half a crown to sup tea with the two-headed lady, and while one head supped the other chatted about the weather, the crowds, and the rip-off prices charged to see the bearded woman next door. "A beard, for heaven's sake! Give me the right injections and I could grow a better beard than that. *Two* beards! What's so good about a beard, I ask you? Confidentially, I think she's a he, anyway."

On Lady Euphemia-Eugenie's advice, he gave the bearded woman a miss. He did hand over another brass coin to watch the waltzing horse, though, but the show wasn't nearly as impressive as he had anticipated.

He sat on a row of benches under a canopy, gazing across the bay to the sweep of land: the beach huts, the town stacked up behind the promenade, the cliffs on the edge of town. Partway up the hill he could see a smudge of dark smoke, and he guessed the school was still smouldering. After he and Grace had left yesterday, apparently, someone had set fire to the main building, and the exposed old beams had gone up like tinder.

That would make rebuilding easier, he thought. The town probably should have a school again. How could they appreciate the freedom, if there was nothing to compare it against?

But they should have a long summer break first of all.

He was the last person sitting on the row of benches.

He stood. Many of the booths – the palm-reader, the photographer, the flea circus – had their boards up now, closed for business, and the rides had stopped their circuits. Most of the music and bells had ceased, and only a few sounds came from further up the pier towards land: the big amusement arcade and the dodgems.

Frankie strolled back indoors and approached the arcade.

Through one of the entrances he saw his father moving about, head down, intent on whatever he was doing. Knots of people still gathered about some of the machines, feeding money in, pulling, nudging. For a moment, Frankie thought they might be mechanicals, but no, they looked real enough. This must be their role, he thought: feeding the machines, keeping the Owner happy. Do that or be wiped away, unwanted. Or live on the fringes like Cindy and her flock of unwanted schoolkids.

He didn't go in. Instead, he ducked down behind the cut-out strong man and waited.

This evening, he was going to wait until the Owner's representative came for the day's takings and then he was going to follow him. No doubt the rep would have other jobs to do after the arcade, other cashboxes to empty, other employees to intimidate, but eventually, Frankie felt sure, the steel-eyed young man in the big suit would lead him to the Owner himself. And *then* Frankie could decide what to do next.

He waited.

He thought back to childhood holidays: Frankie, Grace and their parents. They had been to the Lake District once. Frankie remembered hills towering up over slate-grey lakes, and the sheep dotted about on the rocky slopes like chewing gum on the prom.

They had been to Bournemouth, too, but he hadn't known about the Chinese giant's retirement tea shop then, and so hadn't known to seek it out. It must have been long since closed by then, in any case. Chang Woo Gow had been around in Victorian times, after all.

Sometimes it was hard to recall that there was anything beyond this, anything more than Faraway itself.

Every so often, he peered through the hole in the strong man's face. There were still a few people about, occasionally wandering past either singly or in small groups. Over in the arcade, the punters thinned, until there were only two, feeding coins and pulling at the shiny metal levers.

Father started to cut the power to those gaming machines no longer in use, turning them off at the wall socket in blocks of six to eight. The day was ending. Another day with good takings, Frankie hoped.

The last two left, and Father was on his own. Frankie waited.

"I speak your weight," said a deep voice some time later, as the weighing machine sensed someone passing. "Metric and imperial. And I whisper your body mass index."

Frankie heard footsteps on the wooden boards of the pier. They clacked closer, and then... faded.

Frankie risked a look out of the strong man's face.

Baggy grey suit, short dark hair, and today, a fedora hat with a neat dark ribbon around it.

But... there was something amiss. Something just a little different this time.

Father looked up, with a puzzled expression. "We're just closing, Harry," he said. "Sorry."

The Owner's representative pushed up the brim of his hat. "I've come for the takings, Mickey," he said. "And it better be good."

Frankie knew that voice! It was Barking...

"Sorry?" said Father. "Where's Mr Rosita? He's the one who comes for the takings. Regular as the clock, he is. What are you playing at?"

Mr Rosita must be the Owner's representative, Frankie realised.

Frankie saw Barking grin, then twitch his head to one side to spit gum onto the floor. "Mr Rosita has been unavoidably detained," he said. "You'll be reporting to me from now on, Mickey. What happened is, I became available and it seems the Owner had to find a role for me and this is what he came up with.

"I'm the new representative of the Owner, Mickey me old mucker. I'm da *man*, Mickey. You going to have to please *me* now..."

10. The Children Who Live In Between Places

Frankie didn't follow the Owner's representative after all. Not now that it was Harry Barker, also known as Barking because he liked people to think he was barking mad and just might do almost anything. The Harry Barker who had once smashed Wookie's head between toilet seat and bowl because Wookie had said something about Barking's mum. The Harry Barker who had broken Mr Station's jaw in a tackle in the staff versus pupils rugby match last term. The Harry Barker who was now in charge of Frankie's father. It was hard to accept that he had once considered Barking to be a friend, of sorts.

Frankie sat behind the strong man and thought.

Barking could be dangerous, but then he was working for the Owner, which should restrain him. Frankie doubted Barking would be able to do much against the Owner's wishes, so maybe all this wouldn't be so bad after all. If Frankie tackled the Owner, then he would be tackling Barking too.

The pier was dark now. The area where Frankie hid was lit only by a few flashing neon signs, and lights on some of the machines that had been left on along the walkway: the games where you try to seize a soft toy with a suspended claw, the "I read your fortune" machine, the talking scales.

It seemed wrong for the place to be so quiet. Frankie could hear the waves surging around the footings of the pier, somewhere below the boards.

He emerged from behind the strong man.

"I speak your weight..." said the scales as Frankie walked past.

"Yeah yeah yeah," he said to them, waving a hand dismissively.

He passed the dodgems. The little cars had been parked along the far wall. Someone had swept up, leaving a pile of dirt and stones and litter near the line of dodgem cars.

He came to the swing doors that served both as the entrance and, as Frankie intended now, the exit to the pier. He pushed but was brought up short.

The doors were locked.

Father must have been the last out and he had locked the pier up for the night with his son still inside.

Frankie stood with his face and hands against the glass. He could see the prom, and the decorative gardens with their palm trees and marigolds, and the entrance to Fast Fries.

He waved, trying to attract Mr Singh's attention, but Mr Singh was frying chips and taking money and giving change and those were the things he did. A few people wandered in and out for fish and chips, but Frankie was in darkness, behind two sets of swing doors, and now he remembered how the glass on these doors was sort of mirrored from the outside.

No one saw him.

No one heard him when he called.

He spotted a chair nearby and considered smashing it through the glass. But... well... he couldn't bring himself to do something like that.

He turned, and leaned his back on the locked door. To one side there was an office. There would be a telephone in there. He went across and twisted the door handle, but it too was locked. He went to each of the four pairs of swing doors, in case one had been overlooked, but they were all secured.

He walked back through the covered part of the pier until he emerged in the open. He stood at a railing and looked back along the outside of the pier. There was a narrow gangway leading back towards shore, but he didn't like the look of it and, in any case, he could see from here that there was a metal grille at the end, cutting off access. If they locked up the main doors they were hardly going to leave any other route on or off the pier at night, were they?

He went back inside and found a vending machine. He peered into the gloom at the back and found a socket. When he flipped on the power, the machine lit up. He put some money in and keyed the number for a packet of Doritos.

Munching, he wandered around in semi-darkness, hoping to find a telephone. He knew there was one in the amusement arcade back office, but that, as he had suspected, was locked.

After a time, he returned to the arcade. Switching on a row of six one-armed bandits, he fed a fifty pence piece into the slot of each. He yanked the arm of the first one, then sidestepped to the next and pulled, then the next, and the next until he had the sixth just starting off as the first one slowed.

He pressed Nudge on the first, just as the next machine lit up and klaxoned at him and then spat a handful of coins into its tray. He worked the machines until his change had gone. So much for the evening's entertainments.

He found himself somewhere to settle by the side of the dodgems amongst some old sacking and tarpaulins. Everything smelt of damp. This wasn't exactly the most comfortable bed he had ever found, but it was better than trying to sleep on wooden boards.

He couldn't settle, though. The boards creaked and groaned, the sea surged deep below and every so often a sudden noise from machines still plugged in would startle him – bells, machine voices, strange electronic sound effects. Animal sounds, too: rats and mice, pigeons rustling and crooning, and once a sudden scuttle as an enormous beetle darted across an open area near Frankie's head.

The voices came later. A low murmur of people talking, then a laugh, a squeal, and more low voices.

He heard a klaxon, and then an explosion of change. Someone was in the arcade.

He climbed to his feet, rubbing the sleep from his eyes. He

brushed himself down. He smelt of the musty old sacking now.

Moving cautiously, he stayed close to the wall.

A figure darted into one of the arcade's entrance arches, and then Frankie heard the voices again.

He stopped by the entrance and peered around the Invaders From Mars machine. Just as Frankie had earlier, someone had flipped the power switch for a row of one-armed bandits and they were lit up, flashing, calling.

A girl of about Frankie's age was there, slapping at the buttons, pulling the levers, her face occasionally lit up orange and blue from the machines' lights.

It was Wotsit Cochrane. She'd been with Cindy's group earlier today.

She was good. More often than not, she coaxed cash from the machines and then looked around, startled by the rattle of coins and the celebratory hooting and klaxoning of the machine.

Frankie spotted someone else standing by the girl, watching her, murmuring encouragement.

"*Wookie?*" Frankie said, coming out into the open.

The two looked up, startled.

He went towards them, and when Wookie recognised him the two rushed together and hugged, then separated, embarrassed, clearing their throats with deep, manly rattles of phlegm.

"What's going on?"

Wookie and Cochrane exchanged looks.

"We're just making a bit of money on the machines," Wookie explained. "Ella here's good with them. We never take much. There's never much cash left in them at night." He leaned towards Ella Cochrane and added for her benefit, "Frankie's old man looks after the arcade."

"There's nothing wrong with it," she said. "We're not stealing or nothing. Just playing out of hours."

"But how come you win so often?"

"It's statistics," she explained. "You watch the machines often enough you get to see the patterns, and you know when to nudge, when to spin again. You improve your chances. We're just making enough to get by. There's nothing else for us now school's gone."

Frankie looked away. Okay, he'd made a mistake with school, but did they have to keep reminding him? "How did you get in here?" he asked.

"We live here," said Wookie. "With Cindy and the others. Come on."

Frankie followed the two of them through to the open area by the Thrills Of The Deep Aquarium, pausing only while Ella Cochrane stooped to cut the power to the one-armed bandits. Frankie nodded, approving. At least they were looking after the place. When Ella walked her pockets rattled with change.

Here in the open, there was an octagonal booth that sold rock and candy floss and T-shirts and other seaside tat during the day. Now it was boarded up for the night. Wookie led the way behind it.

The booth backed onto the iron railings which ran along the side of the pier. Wookie swung himself over the edge. For a moment, Frankie thought his friend was going to plunge into the sea, but he caught himself, and then started to climb down.

There was a ladder, Frankie saw. A metal ladder painted black. Ella was waiting for him to go next, so he clambered over the railings, took a deep breath and started to climb.

He never had liked heights. Particularly the kind that were over an angry sea with only your grip on an ancient ladder holding you up. At night. Those kind of heights were among the worst, Frankie decided as he climbed down.

How far?

The sound of the waves seemed awfully near, but he didn't dare look down.

Spray slapped his cheek. It was cold. Wet, too.

He felt hands on his arm.

"Come on," said Wookie. "You're here now."

Here was a wooden platform, suspended below the pier. Frankie couldn't see much, other than the first few planks and the murky cappuccino of Wookie's skin, lit by the moon and the distant lights of the town.

Ella joined them, and Wookie turned. "Mind the step," he said.

Frankie stubbed his toe, then tentatively feeling his way he stepped up onto another level. There was a clank of metal, and he saw Wookie open a metal gate.

"Hey," his friend called. "Cindy. We've got a visitor."

They rounded a corner, and Frankie saw a light flare up as someone turned up an oil lamp. Other lights came up and he looked around.

There was a whole different world down here in the underbelly of the pier. Beams and bars of wood and metal cut across at all kinds of angles, with wooden flooring, and hammocks slung from above. Sheets of corrugated tin had been used to enclose the area, and fishing nets woven with seaweed and other flotsam.

Children were all about. Some could only have been six or seven years old, but most were in their teens. Faces peered from the platforms and hammocks, startled, sleepy, curious.

Cindy stepped out.

"Frankie," she said. "I wondered when you'd find us. I hope you're not going to blab to the Owner and have us tidied away."

"Why would I do that?" asked Frankie. "I want to find him, though. I want to get a few things straight. Do you know where I might find him?"

Cindy shrugged. "I don't know," she said. She started to walk, and Frankie fell into step beside her. "I only ever dealt with his people," she said. "I was just a shop assistant, after all."

She stopped, and faced him. "So," she said, "what do you think of our little hiding place? Have you come to join us?"

"I had no idea there was anything like this beneath the pier," he said.

"I told you there are lots of gaps," she said. "You just need to look. Maybe your Owner's living in one of the gaps, too. All this —" she waved a hand "— used to be storage. And then we added bits to give us a bit more space, make it a bit more homely. You've got to look after these kids. They haven't got anything else now. You haven't answered: have you come to stay with us? You been kicked out, too?"

He shook his head. "How do I get out of here?" he asked. "They'll be wondering where I am."

She put her hands on his shoulders and turned him. There was a gap between a heavy pillar and the concrete edge of the promenade's base. Too narrow, he thought, but when he came to it and turned, he slid through easily enough.

When he looked back from the beach, it was only a dark, shadowy corner. He could barely see the gap at all.

He raised a hand, in case Cindy was still watching, then turned and headed for the steps up onto the prom.

Mother had his dinner on a plate, under a damp tea-towel in the top oven on low to keep it warm and keep the moisture in. It was shepherd's pie, and he could taste the tea-towel on the potato.

"Good day at school?" she asked. Nobody seemed bothered that it was eleven-thirty and he'd only just got home. This really was a world built for Frankie.

"Not bad," he said. "Year Six burnt the main building down, and Mr Witsend was tarred and feathered, and I got a merit in maths. Usual stuff."

Mother tutted. He really was a one.

Grace was still awake when he went up. She was in that Bob the Builder T-shirt that went down to her knees, sitting at her dressing table sticking pressed flowers into a scrapbook.

She used to do that kind of thing all the time.

She smiled a greeting when he came to lean in the doorway.

"Hey, little brother," she said. "Isn't life sweet? Just like it always was, hey?"

He nodded. Just like always. Except...

"I was down at the pier," he said. "Harry Barker's taken over as the Owner's representative down there. He picked up the takings from Father tonight. I don't know what the Owner's playing at. He must know Barking's going to cause trouble! Father has a hard enough time as it is."

"Things will work out, little brother," said Grace, and for a moment he believed her. "Just try not to wade in and change things. We've got it good, Frankie: there's nothing that needs fixing, okay?"

You never win an argument with Grace. That was a rule of the Finnegan household. No point trying.

Particularly when it's past midnight and you're exhausted, after a day when your school's been destroyed and your worst enemy has assumed a position of power over your entire family. On days like that, in particular, it just wasn't worth the effort.

"Night, Sis'," he said.

"Night."

Grace was right. Life *was* sweet. Just like all those long-off memories of days on the beach when there was nothing to trouble your thoughts.

They spent the rest of the week like that. Every morning, Frankie and Grace headed down the steep cobbled streets and through the narrow alleyways to the prom. They would buy crisps and apples on the way, always saving some of their money for later for the stalls and the slot machines and the chip shop.

It was summer forever that week.

On the Thursday they even managed to persuade Mother to accompany them. "We can have a picnic on the beach," Grace told her, "and you can judge sandcastles, even though mine are always best. Frankie can make you some of his clay people from the mud if it's low tide, and we can leave them to dry in the sun while we go to the arcade. You haven't been to the arcade for years!"

They led her to the front door, Frankie holding one hand, Grace the other. On the doorstep she teetered, blinking in the sunlight, like a dormouse emerging from hibernation. "I'm not really sure," she said.

Frankie and Grace were on the pavement, and she stepped down, joining them.

"I'm hardly dressed for an excursion," she said, eyes darting from side to side, up and down the street. She was wearing a long, sagging green cardigan, baggy tracksuit trousers and a pair of fluffy purple slippers.

"You look lovely," said Grace. "Elegant even. Doesn't she, Frankie?"

He nodded. "You look fine," he said.

They walked her down to the high street, pausing to look in the shop windows. It was like showing round a visitor from another country, another planet even. It was as if she'd never seen a greengrocer's or a haberdasher's before.

They sat for a long time on one of the iron benches on the prom, watching the world go past. By this time Mother was smiling, as anyone would, at the atmosphere of fun and relaxation.

On the beach she helped Frankie with his sandcastle, and she grumbled about the sand getting into her slippers.

"Let's go and find Father," said Frankie, early in the afternoon when they had finished their chips and ginger pop.

They climbed the iron steps and went to the pier.

Pushing in through the swing doors, Frankie realised this was the first time he had been here since getting locked in. He wondered if Cindy and the ragamuffins were still living below the planks. He assumed they were.

Mother seemed startled by the dodgems, flinching at each collision, not quite understanding that this was what dodgems *did*. Even before, back when she had been a woman about town, the sea-front and the pier had been alien territory to her.

They came to the arcade.

"Business is good," said Frankie, as they paused at the threshold. The gaming machines were all occupied, flashing and calling to their users. Occasional clatters of coins punctuated the atmosphere, holding out hope for everyone else as they nudged and pulled.

He spotted Father, scurrying about near his cubbyhole office at the far side.

They approached him and when he saw the three of them he paused, surprised. "It's the good lady wife," he said. Then someone nearby slapped, cursing, at the side of a one-armed bandit and Father darted towards him instantly. Glancing over his shoulder, he said, "Apologies, apologies. Duty calls."

He spoke to the man, then reached behind the machine and tweaked at something, before standing back satisfied. Immediately, the punter returned to his gaming.

Father turned, but another bandit crisis called him from across the arcade and he hurried off to assist. Frankie had seen him like this before: you can't interrupt the flow of the game. You wouldn't dare. You had to keep the Owner satisfied. You had to keep the money flowing through.

They waited, but he seemed to have forgotten they were here.

"He's obsessed by those machines," Mother said, dismayed. "He dreams of them, you know. He talks to them when he's asleep."

"Let's go," said Frankie, taking his mother by the arm. Perhaps this hadn't been such a good idea after all.

They passed Father on the way out. He beamed at them and waved a hand. "So what do you think of my little empire?" he said. "Not bad, eh? It certainly buys the biscuits!"

"He could have *been* something in the funeral business," Mother said as they walked back up the pier to the exit. "It's in the family, you know. My father. His father before him. There was an opening for your father if he'd only had the gumption to take it. Those kind of opportunities don't come along every day, you know. He could have been something. There's always a future in funerals."

The next day, Frankie was on his own again. He'd been asking around about the Owner, but wasn't making any progress. They couldn't help him in the library, and the man at the town council offices just gave him a withering look and sent him packing with a few choice comments about wasting the time of Important Town Officials.

He thought again of Cindy's suggestion that the Owner might live like she and her ragged gang did, somewhere in the gaps where no one would normally look.

He hadn't seen her or her followers for a day or two, and with a rush of concern wondered what had become of them. Had they failed to carve out roles for themselves in Faraway as she had feared? Might they have fallen through their gap and gone to somewhere else altogether?

He went towards the pier, then down the steps onto the beach. He studied where the pier joined the prom, but it was all just wooden pillars and metal beams and bolts. He couldn't see the gap. Peering up into the underbelly of the pier, he couldn't work out where there was space for another level where a gang of kids could conceal themselves.

The gaps Cindy talked about must be hard to find, he supposed. You must know exactly how to look for them.

Either that, or Cindy and her gang had been imagined out of existence, their reasons for being here no longer valid. That felt like a great big weight on his shoulders. This was his world. Could people really fade away because their roles had been written out of the script?

He sat on the sand and did his best to remember Cindy and Wookie and the others: the details, the things they said, the way they looked and sounded.

They had been his friends. He had to keep them real.

Frankie wandered up to the pier.

A man in a stripy clown's costume was juggling coconuts by the entrance. As Frankie walked past, the juggler smiled and appeared to forget his act until a coconut crashed down on his head. He did a comical collapse and lay groaning on the floor. People tossed coins into a hat he had placed on the ground.

Frankie planned to go out to that booth and look behind it to see if the ladder was still there. He didn't intend to climb down now, but he needed to know it was still there.

As he walked, he tried to absorb all the details of everything he passed: the tattered edges of the tattoo parlour's signs, the smell of oil and candy floss and brine, the imprint of every passing face. Suddenly he felt terribly responsible for it all.

He passed the arcade, and was pleased to note that the place was as busy as ever. The jangling of coins and bells was a special kind of seaside music, he thought. Like brass bands and barrel organs and the reed pipes of the Punch and Judy show.

He saw Father, over at the Wimbledon tennis video game, polishing away at the display.

Frankie smiled.

And then he hesitated.

There was something about the way Father moved. Something... *precise*. And there was something about the way he gave his complete attention to his current task. His world was wiping that screen at this precise moment.

Frankie went into the arcade. Just as he came within a few paces, his father completed his task, straightened and turned.

He looked at Frankie and the corners of his mouth turned up in what was meant to be a welcoming smile. He dipped his head, and said, "Good... morning... sir. Would you like to play on one of our machines? Change is available from... the booth."

"Father?"

But no, it wasn't.

This... *thing*... looked superficially like Frankie's father. The tone of voice was even similar. But its shiny cheeks with the whiskers crawling down the line of the jaw were too smooth, not real skin at all. And the eyes... they were like the glass eyes of a waxwork doll. They looked like human eyes, they were even the right colour, but there was no life behind them.

"Aaah."

Frankie recognised Barking's voice from behind him immediately. He wondered how long he had been waiting for this moment.

"A family reunion. How touching."

Frankie turned.

Barking stood there chewing gum in the entranceway in his suit that was a size too big, his fedora tipped back on his head.

"What have you done with my father?" demanded Frankie.

Barking smiled and raised his eyebrows. "'Done'?" he asked, all innocence. "We've just been rationalising the business, that's all."

"Where is he?"

Barking shrugged. "Not my responsibility," he said. "He's history as far as I'm concerned. Like footprints in the sand, me old mucker: they always get washed away in the end."

Frankie tried to calm himself.

"So tell me, Finnegan: what do you reckon to the new model?" He nodded towards the mechanical Father, who stood obediently by the video game machine, creepily motionless. "I reckon this is the future. Why pay real people when the mechanicals are just as good? They just blend into the background and no one notices the difference. We don't need real characters at all, a lot of the time, and it's all still pretty convincing."

That wasn't true. What was the world without all the people in it?

Frankie clung onto his father in his head. He remembered him. He believed in him. He would be here somewhere, Frankie just had to go and find him.

Barking wasn't finished though. "This lot –" he nodded towards the mechanical again "– don't cause trouble, for a start. They don't interfere. They don't keep *shifting* things. They don't nose around looking for the Owner. Everything was fine until you started interfering."

"How do you know about what I've been doing?" asked Frankie. He thought of the Important Town Official and the librarian: perhaps one of them had reported him.

But Barking smiled.

"Grace and me," he said, "we agree with each other on this.

You only mess things up when you interfere, Finnegan. You should keep your nose out of where it don't belong."

"*Grace?*"

"She was concerned," said Barking. "So naturally she came to me. And so I decided to tidy your old man out of the picture. You should be grateful that she was looking out for you, Finnegan."

Barking chuckled as Frankie barged past him and out of the arcade.

Just wait until he found Grace and told her what they'd done to Father! This was all her fault.

Father was okay.

Frankie made his way up through the alleyways and cobbled streets to his home. As soon as he entered he heard low voices, conversation from the kitchen.

He went through and there his parents were, sitting at the kitchen table, a pot of tea and two china cups between them.

"I've just come from the pier," said Frankie. "I saw what they've done."

Father nodded, and put his hands around his cup as if they needed warming. "Could be worse, eh?" he said.

"But what will we *do?*" asked Mother.

Misunderstanding, Father replied, "We can spend more time together. Down on the beach, that kind of thing. I spent too long in that place anyway. You always did say."

"No, I mean what will we *do?*"

"Just have to tighten our belts a bit. That's all."

Frankie left them to it.

He went upstairs to the first landing and stopped by Grace's door. It was half open, and she was inside at her desk, sticking down pressed flowers as if she hadn't a care in the world.

"Do you realise what you've done?" demanded Frankie as he stepped into her room. "You and your mate Barking."

She cocked her head on one side and smiled. "He's not my mate, Frankie. He's really rather dull company, if you must know."

"But you blabbed to him, didn't you? You went and told him I was trying to find the Owner."

She stood and turned so that she was resting against the edge of her dressing table, her arms folded across her chest.

"I asked you not to interfere," she said. "I told you it'd only cause trouble. Why mess things up when we have it so good? You, me, Mum and Dad. Everything how we wanted it. How *you* wanted it. Why rock the boat? When I saw you asking all those people about the Owner, well... there didn't seem much point arguing with you again. I'd already tried that."

"You mean you followed me?" Frankie asked.

She shrugged. "I did what I had to."

"And you know what's happened now, I suppose?"

This brought the first shadow of doubt across her features. "What?" she asked.

"Father," said Frankie. "They've kicked him out. Replaced him at the arcade with a mechanical copy. Barking said they'd only done that because you'd gone along interfering with things."

Her jaw worked, but no words came out.

Frankie stepped towards her, pointing his finger. "You complain about *me* interfering, so look what you do! Father's downstairs now, his job just taken away from him. He doesn't have a role any more. Do you know what happens here if you don't have a role?"

"It wasn't me!" hissed Grace. "It was you! You're the one who's interfering. You're the one who's messing things up. If you'd only accepted what we have and been grateful none of this would have happened."

They were standing head to head now, almost touching. Frankie could smell his sister's salty sea-smell, and he could see the grainy texture of her skin.

"It was *you*," he said in a low voice. "You couldn't keep your nose out."

Her eyes were brimming with tears and a muscle tugged at the corner of her mouth.

"You and your mate Harry Barking-Mad..."

One more twitch, then out of the corner of his eye Frankie saw her right arm flash back and then swing, her palm flattened to smack him on the face.

Striking like a snake, he swung his own right hand across and closed his fingers around her wrist.

It felt wrong.

Too soft.

He looked down... gasped.

His fingers had sunk partway into flesh the consistency of dough, of soft clay.

He couldn't feel skin, muscles bone, but instead just an increasing resistance, a thickening of the doughy substance of her arm.

Slowly, he looked back into her face and he saw her as she really was and not as he had so desperately wanted to see her.

Her face was cast from clay, glistening softly in the room's low light. Her eyes were pebbles – flints from the beach. Her hair was the fine trailing seaweed that floated in great drifts in the pools beneath the pier.

She was just like the little clay models he made on the beach and which now littered his room.

Her smell... overpowering now, the smell of the sea, and of the things washed up from the sea.

They stayed like that for a time Frankie was unable to fathom. It felt like hours, but was probably only the merest instant.

He felt tears fill his eyes and the thing before him blurred, and when he blinked she was Grace again. He looked down at where he held her wrist, and saw and felt his fingers being repelled, pushed back out, and he was holding her, just a wrist that felt slightly odd, nothing sinister at all.

"Hold it together, Frankie," she hissed. "Don't lose what we've got. You can't make me go back. I won't let you!"

He let go, and staggered away from her.

He held his hand up in front of his eyes, as if it, or they, had deceived him.

He turned and left the room.

When he looked back, Grace had returned to her pressed flowers.

12. The Boy Who Didn't Know Which Way To Turn

Frankie shut himself in his room.

He had lost his sister again, and it hurt.

He went to the basin in the corner and washed his hands, scrubbing at his right hand with the nail brush until the skin was a livid pink.

He could still feel her flesh giving way under his grip.

She wasn't real, this Grace. She never had been.

She was just... just a *thing*... occupying the space where his sister had once been.

He turned, saw a row of little clay figures on a shelf, and he swung his arm wildly, sweeping them to the floor.

He sat back on his bed and rested his chin on his knees.

He didn't have anywhere to turn. This was Faraway, the world of his daydreams. Where else was there?

"Dinner!" Mother bellowed up the stairs. She had a big voice for a small woman. Had she always had such a big voice, or was that some kind of a flaw in this world...?

Frankie looked around his room. Everything seemed to be right. The curled-back corner of wallpaper in the corner by the door. The stacks of tatty old paperbacks on top of his chest of drawers. The thermometer set into a little anchor hanging from a nail on the far wall.

If the details could be right in Faraway, why was it that the important things were so very wrong?

He went downstairs.

Grace and Father were already at the table. Mother turned from the cooker, smiling. "As we're all here, I thought we could have a sit-down dinner," she said. "Your father's usually..." She turned back to her cooker.

Frankie's father was usually at work.

Frankie sat. He stared at the surface of the table. He couldn't bring himself to look at Grace or his parents. That would have been too much.

"I've been out again," said Mother, placing plates before them all. "I've been to the convenience store to buy this."

There were three slices of pink meat on Frankie's plate. Some kind of processed meat loaf, he suspected.

She placed dishes of potatoes, leeks and peas on the table, and a small china jug of gravy.

Frankie prodded at the meat on his plate, while the others helped themselves from the dishes. "Potatoes, Frankie?" asked Father. "They look like Jersey Royals, is that right, good lady wife?"

Frankie shook his head. "I'm not hungry," he croaked.

"We need to feed you up," said his mother, leaning across to pinch his cheek. "You'll waste away, you will."

He reached up and grabbed her wrist. Squeezed.

He felt bone, tendons, loose skin.

Mother jerked her hand back. "Hey!" she said. "That hurt!"

The feel of real flesh and bone was almost more shocking than if her wrist had been soft and yielding.

"What you doing, boy?" demanded Father. "You apologise, you hear?"

"Sorry, Mother," Frankie mumbled.

Then he pushed his chair back and rose. "I'm going to bed," he said. "I'm tired."

His parents just stared at him, looking puzzled at his behaviour.

Grace smiled her same old smile. "Night, little brother," she said. "See you tomorrow."

In the morning he went straight down to the front door. He

didn't fancy breakfast. He didn't want to face people.

Grace was waiting for him outside.

She had chalked a hopscotch grid onto the pavement, and as he opened the door she was hopping from square to square.

She looked up and smiled.

"Shall we go to the beach this morning, Frannie?" she asked, just like a normal day. "We could build sandcastles – maybe build one together, then you won't be bothered 'cos mine's always best."

That look in her eye. Pleading with him. He thought of all the sunny blue-skied days they had spent on that beach. Maybe things would work themselves out.

He turned away.

No! What was he thinking?

She was a lump of mud.

"Don't be too quick to judge me," she said, coming to stand before him. "You need to *try*, Frannie. We all need you to try. Don't stop believing."

He wouldn't meet her look.

"Is this what you want, Frannie?"

He looked now. He watched her dry up before his eyes, moist clay setting, eyes turning to stone. She started to crumble to the ground, lumps breaking away, turning to dust.

She was a heap before him on the ground. Dirt and seaweed and a scattering of stones.

From somewhere, her voice came again: "Is this what you want?"

He stepped around her, and headed for the high street.

They had all come off the train. Day trippers with picnic hampers marched down the hill from the station, ready for another day out by the sea. They called and laughed as their children chased balls down the road and played tag among the crowds.

Frankie was the only person heading in the other direction.

He came to the old red-brick station building, with its neat white wicket fence and its hanging baskets bursting with geraniums and lobelia. You had to go through the building to get onto the platform, so he opened the door and went into the echoing foyer.

The ticket hatch had its blind pulled down and a handwritten notice that said "Closed. Please buy your ticket on the train."

He went through.

A train was due in a few minutes, so he found a bench and sat.

Frankie was lost. He didn't know what to do, but what he did know was that he couldn't bear to be in the same house as that *thing* that was pretending to be his sister.

Grace was dead. She had died two years ago when a Volvo shattered her skull on the high street.

That thing was just a pile of mud in the street.

He had to get away. He had to escape, just like he always ended up having to escape.

He peered along the track. It was misty along there and the rails faded into greyness. He wondered where they led.

He heard a rhythmic rattle from the tracks, then a hoot, and the huffing of a steam engine. It came out of the mist, slowing already. It was a massive barrel-shaped engine, with a flaring chimney stack belching clouds of steam. Its dark green paintwork was immaculate, and the metal trim gleamed as if someone had been up all night with the Brasso.

Brakes squealed as it came to a halt, its three carriages lined up along the platform.

Windows slid down and hands reached out to release the doors, and then people spilled out.

Frankie stood back while the train emptied, then he approached one of the doors. A man in dark blue uniform barred his way. "Ticket?" he said.

"Yes, please," said Frankie, fumbling for his money. "Where does the train go?"

"No," said the man. "You have to have a ticket valid for your journey if you wish to embark."

Frankie stared at him. "But..." he said. "The ticket office is closed. It says to buy tickets on the train."

"You can't get on without a ticket valid for your journey," said the man.

"Then can I buy a ticket, please?"

"Certainly," said the man. "Ticket office is that way."

Frankie sighed. He wasn't going to get anywhere like this. He turned away, and went along to the last carriage. The door was open. Frankie put his foot on the step –

"Ticket?"

It was the same man.

"I..."

"You have to have a ticket valid for your journey if you wish to embark," said the man.

Frankie backed away.

He watched as the stationmaster walked along the platform, slamming the train's doors, then stood back and blew a whistle. Slowly, the train hauled itself away from the station.

Frankie waited until it had gone, then went back through the station building past the closed ticket hatch and out into the street.

The path ran between the railway track and the town allotments for a short distance. The ground was uneven and damp and Frankie had to watch out for dog mess, but at least that gave him something to occupy his mind.

To his left, wigwams of runner beans were covered with crimson blossoms, peas scrambled over twiggy supports, and onions stood bulging out of the ground in neat rows. Ramshackle sheds with shiny padlocks huddled at the end of each strip and a lone old woman stooped over a hoe, dragging at the earth of her immaculate plot.

Fingers of mist clung to the hillside on the far side of the tracks. The sky was a featureless grey, a thick haze cutting out clouds and sun.

Frankie walked on.

He couldn't remember how far it was to the next town, but if he didn't get there today then he would sleep rough and resume his journey in the morning.

The end of the allotments was marked by a high hawthorn hedge heavy with white blossom. There was a rough field beyond, with a horse and foal in a distant corner. The footpath still followed the line of the railway, which suited Frankie well.

After he had been walking for some time – half an hour at least, he felt; he didn't have a watch – he heard the eerie screeching whistle of a train. A dark shape emerged from the mist ahead, and then almost instantly it was rushing past him with a loud roar and rattle and hiss, and a blast of hot air.

And then it was gone, and he was alone again.

The ground on Frankie's side of the track had opened out now. It was rough, covered in tussocks of spiky grass and small clumps of bramble. He couldn't see any sign that the ground was divided into fields: no hedges, no fencing.

On the far side of the track... it was hard to see through the thickening mist. The hill still seemed to loom on that side, with dark shapes that must be trees.

The path was nothing now. There hadn't really been a path for a while. But he could still walk across the rough ground, keeping the railway to his right so that he wouldn't lose his way. It was as good as having a path, kind of. That's what he told himself.

Another train rushed past, billowing steam. It was like some kind of legendary beast, he thought: an iron dragon.

He stopped and rested, sitting on the flat stump of a tree. He had a Twix in his pocket, and he ate one of the sticks, then folded the other in the wrapper and tucked it away for later.

He was thirsty now. He should have brought a can. There

were all kinds of things he should have brought, if only he'd planned this a bit more thoroughly. Like a map. Or even a train ticket.

Standing, he peered into the gloom. For a moment, all he saw was greyness and this made him dizzy.

He fixed his eyes on the ground, and the old stump, and slowly his head stopped spinning.

He couldn't see the railway line any more.

The stump. The stump had been on Frankie's right when he came to it, which meant the rails had been just beyond. He stood with the stump on his right and stared into the fog.

There was just flat, rough ground all about him.

He determined not to panic yet. Save that for later. Panic really needed building up to, after all.

The sun. In ancient times they had navigated by the sun and the stars – if they could see them, of course.

The sun was a brighter patch on the grey sky.

He closed his eyes and thought. The sun had been over his left shoulder when he had set out, and the railway had followed a straight line.

He turned so that the slightly brighter patch of sky was behind his left shoulder and the stump still to his right, and then he started to walk. Only an amateur needed a railway line to follow.

Almost immediately, there was a sudden eruption at his feet and a dark shape burst out and upwards from a tussock.

A bird. A pigeon or something.

Frankie gathered himself, checked the position of the sun, and resumed his trek.

A few minutes later, a harsh whistle tore through the still air.

He heard the huffing of a steam engine, and the rattling roar of steel wheels on steel track.

He stopped, struggling to fix the direction, as the sounds grew louder.

A sudden rush of panic –

He looked down at the ground, and sobbed a sigh of relief. For an instant he had thought he might have wandered onto the rails themselves, but no, he stood on turf cropped short by rabbits.

The sound faded. He heard one last, distant, whistle and then nothing more.

Frankie sank to his knees, and looked all around.

Fog clung to the rough ground.

Every direction looked the same.

Somewhere high up he heard a gull cry: a long screech followed by "eck-eck-eck-eck" as if the bird was laughing at him.

He climbed to his feet, turned so that the brighter patch of sky was at his left shoulder, and resumed his march.

Ahead, the fog appeared to be thinning.

Frankie didn't know how long he had been walking, but now he quickened his stride.

The ground rose a little and he stumbled, but kept going.

And then the ground before him vanished.

He caught himself, with one foot in mid-air where ground should have been.

He stumbled back and ended up sitting on the mud, heart pounding, mouth dry.

Just in front of him the ground stopped.

He listened and heard waves somewhere far below. He had come out at the top of a cliff. He tried to recall the map of the local railway line so that he could work out where this would be, but it evaded him.

With his breathing almost back to normal, he looked around. The fog was definitely thinning. The clifftop stretched away to his right, but to his left it dropped steadily. There must be a cove there, or maybe a river valley.

As he watched, the fog thinned even more, and down below he saw the first in a line of beach huts and the beginning of a stone promenade.

Sun broke through, and Frankie saw further along the line of beach huts to the first brightly coloured buildings of a town, huddled close together on the steeply rising ground behind the beach.

He was looking out over a wide bay, cut in two by the long straight line of a pier.

He was looking back at his home town, but he hadn't really come home: this town had been rearranged, distorted by the workings of his own imagination.

He had come back to Faraway.

13. In Which The Finnegans Begin Again

Frankie tried to get his bearings. The railway line led directly inland from the station and yet... He had followed it, only losing his way for the last short stretch of the trek, and now he found himself where the cliffs started just to the south of town.

He had come almost a full circle, while walking in a straight line away from town.

That wasn't possible.

But then, Faraway itself wasn't possible, yet it *was*. It existed. The place spread out before him, its colours vibrant in the sunlight.

He turned away from the view.

A rough path led along the clifftop in the other direction, but in only a short distance it was lost in a wall of grey. The fog ebbed and surged, reaching towards him then drawing back like waves on the beach.

He remembered how he had come so close to stepping over the edge. He wondered how far he would get along the clifftop before he came to another drop and this time, perhaps, wouldn't be able to stop himself from plunging over.

He turned back towards town and began to walk.

He hadn't given up yet, though. After a short time he came to a sequence of steps cut into the gentle slope of the cliff-face. They were uneven and damp from the fog, so he had to watch his step with care, but soon he reached the bottom.

On the beach, he turned away from town once again.

The fog closed in around him, but he kept going. The tide was low, so he could walk on damp sand, which was easier. He always kept an eye on the high-tide line, though, making sure that he would have safe ground to retreat to when the tide came in.

The fog didn't matter so much here. All he had was the mud and sea on his left, and the rocks and cliff on his right. He couldn't get lost, and he didn't have to see far.

Frankie sat out high tide on a stack of rocks at the foot of the cliff. It looked as if the land had slumped here and an entire block of stone had slid down the cliff-face.

He ate the remaining finger of Twix. The combination of chocolate and biscuit made him thirsty. He searched among the rocks until he found a pool of water. He dabbed a finger in and tasted it cautiously, expecting it to be salty, but it was okay. He was high enough above the spray line that this must be captured rainwater, or it might even have condensed from the fog that never cleared.

Cupping his hands into the water, he drank. It tasted strange: earthy, sharp. He hoped it wouldn't make him ill, but he drank more even so. He had to drink.

He set out again, as the tide began to ebb, but soon it was growing dark. He found shelter under a rocky overhang, and then proceeded to gather dry weed and other debris – anything that was soft enough – to protect him from the hard edges of the rocks.

He had been walking all day, but actually, to his surprise, he felt quite good. He couldn't remember the last time he had pushed himself physically like this.

Sunlight woke Frankie after a night when he hadn't expected to sleep at all.

For a few seconds he was confused and couldn't work out where he was and why the ground was so hard, then it came back to him. For a second or two more he believed that the fog had lifted: he could see the rocks around him, and the morning sun felt so warm! But no, he was still engulfed in grey.

Frankie set off again, thirsty and hungry and stiff.

A short time later he was convinced that the fog really was lifting. The sun on his aching back felt good!

He walked on wet sand, aware that the sea was not far to his left and he would have to scramble up to the dry rocks before long.

Soon, the sand was just a narrow strip between the sea and a straight line of rock.

He turned and stepped up onto a lump of stone, then pulled himself up another until he stood on a flat surface. He studied the ground: this wasn't a natural slab of stone, it had been carved out, shaped.

The edge of the stone shelf on which he stood stretched out ahead, a perfect straight line. He saw now that the surface was not stone: it was concrete.

He walked, and the fog thinned.

To his right, the first beach hut appeared. It was rather shabby and didn't look as if it had been used for some time, the white paint peeling, the door's padlock rusted into place. Next door there was another hut, painted yellow with a white door, better maintained than its neighbour. The next along was blue, then yellow again, then white.

He walked along the prom. A wrought-iron railing appeared, guarding the drop to the beach below, and gas lamps on black metal posts now appeared at regular intervals.

Ahead, the pier cut across the bay and on the prom the trees of the ornamental gardens sprang up.

Frankie was coming into town from the other side. By some quirk of geometry he had gone full circle again.

His shoulders slumped, his eyes stung, his body ached. He kept walking.

There was no escape from Faraway.

He should have known.

Not long afterwards, Grace joined him.

She fell into step at his side, as if she had been waiting.

They walked in silence for a time, in the morning sun. It was just as if they had been off exploring along the beach, as they had done so many times in the past.

"You cool, Frannie?"

"I'm cool," he said.

It was still early and the town was only just coming to life. They came to the small harbour, where fishermen sat mending the nets all bunched up at their feet or doing mysterious things with crab and lobster pots. Down below the harbour wall, a young man hauled boxes of iced fish out of a squat fishing boat and handed them to a woman who stacked them nearby.

They came to the part of the gardens where Frankie had first paid attention to this Grace: a girl with something different about her in the crowd at the Punch and Judy show.

"Remember when I bought you that silly anchor thermometer you keep on your wall?" Grace asked him. "You liked the anchor, but you didn't like the thermometer bit at first, until you understood what it was."

Frankie smiled and nodded. "Then I took to checking every ten minutes to see if it had become warmer or cooler." He glanced at her, and there was life in her eyes. He would play the game. He would try. "Do you remember how I used to read you stories when we were little and I could read better than you?" he asked.

"I had to learn to read for myself because I hated all those gruesome ghost stories you used to read. Do you remember how we used to shut ourselves in your room and imagine strange worlds while Mum and Dad fought downstairs? Because they did: they fought even before the accident – they didn't split up just because of me..."

He remembered.

"Still," Grace said now. "We're all back together again at last, aren't we?"

He nodded. You've got to have a dream, as the old song went. Otherwise, how's it ever going to come true?

The dispossessed had gathered on the beach around the pier, scattered across the sand in small groups. Their clothes were filthy rags, and they had their possessions in bundles on the sand.

Frankie stood on the prom and surveyed the scene. He couldn't see Cindy or Wookie or Ella Cochrane or any of the kids that had formed part of their group. They would be somewhere, though. He couldn't accept that they might have been wiped out. They were still very real to Frankie.

"Over there," said Grace, pointing.

Their parents sat together. Mother wore her tracksuit bottoms, cardigan and fluffy purple slippers again. Father was in grubby jeans and a scuffed leather coat with no shirt, as he sat with his knees drawn up, his whole body rocking back and forth. They had nothing with them other than what they wore.

Frankie and Grace went down and sat with them.

"What happened?" asked Frankie. "Why are you down here on the beach like this?"

"They haven't got a home," said Grace. "Things aren't stable up there anymore. There have been too many upheavals."

"Just need to get my old job back, eh?" said Father, glancing at Frankie and giving a brief smile. "That's all it needs. I'll go back, cap in hand. I'll take a pay cut. I'll work longer hours. Whatever he wants. Just enough to keep us in biscuits, that's all I ask."

"That place," hissed Mother, glowering up at the pier. "Your father thinks it'll solve everything: just go back and look after those bloomin' machines!"

Father was still rocking back and forward.

"We need to start over," said Mother. "Find a new place, a new reason to be here."

"You have every reason to be here," said Frankie. "You're our parents. You don't need any other role."

But they needed somewhere to live.

He remembered what it had been like when all this had been fresh and new. He remembered *imagining* a creek stopping Barking and Stu from catching him. He remembered *imagining* the town with hunched up cobbled streets and gas lamps just like the Faraway he and Grace had always talked about. He remembered *imagining* that school would no longer intrude on their idyllic summer holiday lives.

"No, Frannie," said Grace at his side. "Not anymore."

Frankie stood and turned. He climbed up to the promenade, and walked through the alleyway to High Street.

His family needed a home.

He closed his eyes and wished. He tried to remember how it had felt to seize control of this world and reshape it. He tried to recreate the shifting sensation in his head, in his gut – and translate that into the world around him.

He didn't think it would come. His grip had slipped.

He kept his eyes squeezed tightly shut and tried to direct everything within him into reshaping the world.

He felt as though he would burst.

And then the ground shuddered, and he both heard and felt the groan that reached up through his body and squeezed tight.

Something bucked and flipped beneath his feet and he opened his eyes. The paving slab he stood on had tipped up, and as it shifted again he stumbled forward onto his knees, unable to stay upright.

Somewhere in the distance he heard shouts and cries, but that didn't matter.

In front of him, right in the middle of High Street, stood a cottage. Its walls were built from tiny red bricks, smoothed and rounded with age. Shutters were latched open at each window, and a pink rose rambled over a frame around the door.

All around this newly emerged building, the cobbled road rose in great ripples, as if someone had thrown a rock in a pond and the splash had been frozen as it spread. Buildings nearby had tipped up and long cracks spread over their walls.

He crossed the uneven ground and approached the front door. He slid his key into the lock. It turned easily.

He didn't go inside. Instead, he turned, and called, "Mother? Father? It's okay. You have a home again. You have that little cottage you always talked about. It's just how you described."

He headed back through the alleyway to the prom, but when he got there he found everything in chaos. Giant slabs of stone and concrete tipped at all angles, and the iron railings were twisted and broken where the upheavals had pulled them apart.

Someone lay full-length across one slanting lump of promenade, a hand reaching into a hole in the ground, talking to whoever was down there.

The ground rumbled again, and Frankie staggered out into the open. He looked up at Buckets And Spades and saw that the entire shop had ridden a ripple in the ground and now leaned at an improbable angle towards the sea. At any moment it might tip right over.

Frankie edged away.

Other buildings had tipped and bucked, walls sagging, bearing loads in directions they had never been called on to do before.

Down on the beach, the dispossessed mingled with day-trippers, all staring back at the town in disbelief.

Frankie spotted Grace and their parents among the bemused onlookers. He scrambled over the uneven slabs of promenade and down onto the beach.

"Look what you've done!" hissed Grace. "I *told* you!"

He ignored her.

"Father, Mother," he said. "It's okay. You have a home again. Your cottage."

Father sat there rocking, and Mother looked from one to the other.

"Let's get you back home," said Frankie. "A nice cup of tea."

That's what you need." Mother took his outstretched hand and pulled herself to her feet. She put a hand on Father's shoulder and said something close to his ear. He stood, and the two of them went with Frankie.

Grace trailed after them, but wouldn't come in.

"No," she said. "You're tearing the world apart, Frannie. Look!" She pointed.

Frankie looked up the hill. A heavy mist had settled, cutting across the cobbled High Street about halfway up. He shook his head. The mist would lift when the day warmed up. A bit of sunshine was needed, that was all. He opened the cottage door and ushered his parents inside.

The kitchen stove was burning well, but he put a couple more logs on anyway. Then he lifted a big black kettle onto the hot plate and waited for it to boil.

He looked around the little kitchen, with its pine shelves and the sun slanting in through the small window.

They had made a start, he thought. A new start.

14. Trying To Keep All Of The Bricks In The Air

Frankie had been right. All his parents needed was a cup of tea and everything would be okay.

A tin of Darjeeling was there in the well-stocked pantry, and a big white teapot stood ready on the first shelf of the Welsh dresser.

They drank the tea Frankie made, and steadily their spirits rallied.

"Look!" gasped Mother, pointing at the row of photographs hanging from one wall. Father as a young man, balancing a toddler on each shoulder. The two of them on their wedding day, with confetti showering down. Frankie and Grace sharing a donkey ride at some seaside resort. That had to be somewhere else, Frankie knew, for they had never ridden the donkeys here.

People are like that: they go away just so they can do things they really could have done on their own doorstep.

He looked at his parents, and wished they could be like this again all the time.

The cottage's front room had a suite of upright chairs and a sofa, all upholstered in a fabric patterned with roses, matching those that grew around the front door. Glinting horse brasses hung from nails on the heavy wooden beams that supported the ceiling. Toby jugs laughed and gurned from any available shelf or niche.

It was just like the cottage interiors in the magazines Mother would hoard. Frankie was sure this place was exactly what she had always dreamed of.

They sat in the rose-clad seats, peaceful, oblivious to the horse-drawn coaches struggling to manoeuvre around this house newly-sprung from the centre of the high street.

It needed a "Home Sweet Home" plaque to hang from one of the walls, but nothing else.

They spent the day enjoying the new house, and pottering in the small back garden, dead-heading the flowers and gathering snails and slugs to toss over the back wall. For the evening meal, Mother roasted a small chicken, with potatoes and parsnips.

Grace had abandoned them, it seemed. She had warned Frankie not to push for any more changes in Faraway, so to come into the cottage might mean she was accepting that she had been wrong.

She would relent eventually, and then she would see how peaceful it was here.

During the day Frankie did his best to ignore the faint groans and tremors from deep in the ground. Wherever possible, he avoided looking out beyond the boundaries of the family cottage, too. He didn't want to know.

In the evening they played backgammon, Frankie teaching his parents the rules.

In the night, he felt more upheavals, too substantial to ignore.

By morning he knew that this had only been a temporary respite. In the kitchen, plates and cups had fallen from their places on the dresser, and the floor was strewn with shattered china. Down on her hands and knees with a dustpan and brush, Mother smiled up at Frankie as he entered.

"Good morning, Frankie," she said, struggling to stay upbeat. "I'm afraid we'll be using the second best china today."

In the back garden, pots had tipped over, spreading dark compost over the slabs. At the far end, the garden wall had buckled, and a number of bricks had fallen. Frankie turned and saw a jagged crack slanting across the whitewashed back wall of the house.

This was never going to last.

"I'll be back later," he called to Mother, as he let himself out of the gate at the end of the garden and stepped into the middle of the high street.

He needed to find somewhere safe for his parents. Cindy knew about safe places, if only she was still around. If he could track her down she would help. And once he had found refuge for his parents, he needed to tackle the Owner.

He crossed the road and entered one of the alleyways that led through to the promenade. He had to watch his footing at every step, with the slabs tilted and the cobbles loose and slippery with moisture from the damp air.

He paused to look up the hill. The fog was closer today. He wondered how long he might have left.

In the alleyway, Frankie staggered as a slab moved under his foot. He caught himself against a wall, and at that instant he felt the earth groan again.

He watched as the alleyway distorted, stretching itself out. The buildings to either side tipped closer together until their walls butted against each other a little above the first floor. Gaps opened up between paving slabs, soil and dark cavities in between.

He stepped forward and the ground lurched again.

The walls were even closer together now.

He pressed on, ducking down to squeeze through the gap remaining between the two buildings.

Another upheaval and he was on his knees, struggling to catch the breath that had been knocked out of him.

He peered back, wondering what was happening to the cottage during all this, but the buildings blocked his view. He tried to get up, but his shoulders struck the leaning walls – now much closer together – and he sagged down again.

He crawled, on paving slabs that shifted under his weight, between walls that inched and bulged and tipped.

At the end, he collapsed on the prom, and when he looked back there was only the merest of gaps between the two buildings, too tight even for a cat to slip through.

He peered along the sea front. It was as if a bomb had struck. Lots of bombs. Each of the great stone blocks of the prom had tilted at a slightly different angle, and gas lamps jutted and dangled, some broken in two.

A man in a stripy blazer and a straw boater with a broken brim sat determinedly on an iron bench, licking at a double ninety-nine. Further along a performer with painted face and bell-strewn hat juggled half-bricks with a fixed grin on her face.

Somewhere, a brass band played "Oh I do like to be beside the seaside".

Frankie struggled over the heaved-up prom and lay on his belly, looking out across the beach. A mixture of dispossessed town folk and trippers were scattered across the sand, just as the day before, but he couldn't see his friends.

He rolled onto his back and sat up. The town seemed to loom over him, accusing, threatening.

"Cindy!" he called. "Wookie!"

Faces turned towards him, and he didn't like their angry expressions, so he fell quiet again.

He tried to think rationally. If Cindy and her gang had survived – and they *must* have – then she would have found another gap, a secret place like the storage area under the pier.

He sighed.

How was he ever going to find somewhere like that?

He tried coming at the problem from another direction.

If she was hiding, then who was she hiding from? This was Frankie's world, although the Owner and his people might dispute that. So presumably she was hiding in a gap that was hidden... from Frankie and the Owner...

He was only ever going to find her if she wanted to be found, he realised. Which wasn't a lot of help for him now.

He went down to the beach, collecting a piece of broken railing on his way. On the wet sand, he scratched a message in letters as tall as he was himself:

CINDY HELP – FRANKIE

It would only last as long as people's scuffing feet or the returning tide would allow, but it had to be worth a try.

He went back up to the prom and worked his way along, wary of the ground shifting beneath his feet.

He tried hard to remember the prom as it had been: the hard, flat, concrete surface, the railings, all the buoyant, happy people. That seemed to work for a while, or at least, things didn't get any worse.

The pier was better, but he couldn't bring himself to go far. He didn't want to see the mechanical replacement for his father in the amusement arcade. He looked down at the base of the pier, but couldn't see Cindy's gap.

He came to the Krazy Golf course, where the ground looked like a rug someone had ruckled up on a polished floor. No one was trying to play, although Mr Woods still stood in his booth with the clubs and the balls and the scorecards just in case.

Frankie walked around the outside of the Krazy Golf until he came to the big palm tree that marked the start of the ornamental gardens. Its bristly trunk was tipping over to one side now.

Someone was standing behind it.

Frankie circled the tree slowly. A man stood there, very upright, wearing white trousers, a navy blue blazer and a white seaman's cap. He had thick grey whiskers down his jaw and a crooked pipe hanging from one corner of his mouth. He looked like a shop-window mannequin, or one of the mechanicals switched off, awaiting instruction. But no: he was real all right. A second or two after Frankie found him, his eyes snapped sideways, locking on Frankie. He smiled, revealing yellow teeth.

It was the Jolly Old Sea Captain, the figure of so many childhood nightmares.

Frankie stepped back, catching his heel on a paving slab.

The sea captain jerked away from the tree and turned stiffly.

Frankie managed to find his feet again without falling. He turned and ran.

But the going wasn't easy, with the ground so broken up.

Every time he glanced back, the Jolly Old Sea Captain was there, his stiff-bodied walk somehow well-suited to the rough terrain.

Frankie ran and fell, scrambled to his feet again and ran. Back out onto the prom, and along past the pier.

He had been heading for the alleyway, but of course it had rearranged itself and was no longer passable. He skidded to a halt and looked around.

The man in the stripy blazer still sat on his bench, his ice-cream gone now. Further along, the juggler still performed, keeping five half-bricks in the air and a smile on her face.

And still, the Jolly Old Sea Captain came.

Something nagged away at Frankie, more than the sense that he had been here before. He had been pursued by the old sea captain in so many nightmares, after all.

He heard the old sea captain laugh and he knew that voice from somewhere.

He ran over tipped slabs, disturbing the juggler so that first one brick and then all the others crashed to the ground.

He darted in between two beach huts, then along to the narrow gully behind them and scrambled along, before stepping back into the gap between two huts further along.

He peered out, and saw the Jolly Old Sea Captain ambling about on the wrecked prom, confused, lost.

As he passed nearby, Frankie finally recognised him: Mr Cray! So this was what had become of their teacher when the school had closed... Unlike so many of the pupils, there had been a ready-made role for Mr Cray: town bogeyman.

"Help," the old captain mumbled, heading back towards the pier. "You have to help us, Finnegan."

Frankie ducked back into his hiding place until the creature had gone.

He was *trying* to help. Trying to help them all.

But everything was falling apart... How could he hold it all together? He tried so hard to believe in it all, but that wasn't enough.

If he had ever had any kind of grip on Faraway, he had lost it now.

Much later, Frankie picked his way back along the prom. Things appeared to have calmed down a little now. He hadn't felt the ground shift for much of the day and, as he walked, the slabs were stable, not wobbling and sliding about as if they were trying to throw him at every step.

The day-trippers were making the best of it all, as they tended to do. They queued for hot dogs, they spread picnic blankets on the sand, they played frisbees amongst the rubble. The sun shone down on them, like a heavenly pat on the back.

Frankie came to where the alleyway had been and then went further along to the next opening.

He hesitated.

Then he stepped into the narrow space. Nothing shifted. Nothing bucked or swayed.

He walked along the alleyway and emerged on the high street.

Standing on the cobbles he was struck by the sense of quiet. There were no people here, no rushing carriages, no rats scuttling around the rubbish bags, no stray dogs strutting and sniffing.

Mist fingered the far side, greying everything.

He looked up the slope towards the cottage. It still stood, but the fog reduced it to a dark grey block.

Frankie hurried.

The mist thinned a little as he approached, but he knew this building was lost to it.

The front door hung open, and there was every sign that this house was long abandoned. Even so, Frankie went inside and called, "Mother? Father? Is anyone there?"

Cobwebs clung thickly to every surface, and the musty smell of dust and decay was thick in the air. In the kitchen, all the metal fittings were scabbed over with rust, and when he opened the pantry door he staggered back from the smell of rotten food.

He went from room to room, and everything was broken, filthy, decayed.

He left the house, emerging in thick fog.

For a few seconds he had no sense at all of where he was, and then he determined the direction of the slope and staggered downhill, through mist that thinned, towards the prom.

He couldn't keep it together.

He couldn't keep this place together at all.

15. The Misguided Individual Who Still Held Out Hope And The One Who Put An End To It

Frankie went back through to the prom. There didn't seem to be anywhere else to go, with the fog closing in as it was.

He made it across the prom, and climbed down a sloping block of concrete to the beach. At least the ground here was flat. Others had done likewise. Most of the town now seemed to have taken up residence on the beach.

Faces turned to Frankie as he passed.

He wouldn't meet anyone's look. They all knew. They all blamed him.

He wandered from group to group. Where he recognised someone he asked, "Have you seen my parents? Have you seen Cindy from the corner shop, or Wookie Trew, or Ella Cochrane?"

In response: shakes of the head, shrugs, or just blank, lost looks.

His parents had a beach hut now.

He found them after a long time wandering around among the lost on the beach. Down here, a long stretch of promenade had tipped over completely, and a row of beach huts had been dumped on the sand. Many of them were wrecked, many more were at least partly broken and collapsed, while one or two had been transplanted whole, as if they were really meant to be on the beach and not up on the prom.

His parents sat by one of the partly-broken huts. One end of the hut had collapsed, tipping the front end back at a jaunty angle. It was still possible to open the door and find shelter in what remained of this ruined hut.

When Frankie found them, they had propped the door open. Mother sat in the doorway, while Father sat nearby.

He leapt to his feet when Frankie approached.

"Things are looking up, eh, Frankie? We've found ourselves a place to stay." He waved his hand to indicate the slumped beach hut. "And I've resolved myself to go up to the pier and ask for me old job back. There's room here for you and Gracie, too, of course. Then everything'll be right with the world again, won't it?"

Frankie stared at his dirty, unshaven father. He looked at the wrecked beach hut, at mother squatting sullenly in her open doorway, at the ruined sea-front beyond.

He looked at his father again. How could he still cling to hope amid all this?

"Father," he said. "Your job has gone, you've lost your home, and Grace is dead. I'm sorry, but that's how it is."

Father stared at him, and in her doorway Mother gave a soft little sob.

"Grace?" asked Father.

Frankie nodded, and the two stepped forward into each other's arms.

"She died two years ago, didn't she, Father? You remember, don't you?"

Father nodded against Frankie's shoulder. "She ran off," he said. "She wouldn't stop. She told me to go to hell and she ran off and I didn't think any more of it because she was like that and she'd cool down. Just like always. And I was at work, anyway. Couldn't desert me post, could I?"

"I was there too," said Frankie tentatively. "Remember? On the prom. I saw her come running out and I tried to stop her, but I couldn't."

Grace – the real, live, wild-like-a-cornered-animal Grace – had been like a force of nature.

Some of the time she was the calmest, most peaceable child

you could imagine, and she and Frankie had spent long days together – the kind of days you would always cherish.

But at other times... She had a temper that crackled like hot cooking oil, and she seemed to want to turn against everything and everyone. She had run with Barking's gang and got in trouble with school and the police and she wouldn't listen to anyone.

She was good at heart, though. She was *Grace*.

That day... Frankie remembered seeing her come running out of the pier and he knew she had been fighting with Father again.

"Grace!" he had called. She stopped, and just for an instant he thought he had broken through and she was going to cool down.

Then her eyes had narrowed and her upper lip had curled in a sneer and she had spat back at him, "Button it, Fran. Just keep your filthy nose out of it, okay?"

"But..."

"Stop interfering, little brother, okay?" She had winked, and at that moment a flash of understanding had passed between the two of them: she wasn't mad at him, wasn't even really mad at Father for whatever row the two of them had had. It was just a role she was trapped in. She was the wild child: she had to fight back even when there was no one to really fight.

She ran.

Frankie had watched her dart out through the ornamental gardens to where they joined the high street.

He didn't see what happened next, but he heard the squeal of brakes, the muffled thud, the exclamations of those nearby, and then a small child crying inconsolably.

Now, he held his sobbing father in his arms and thought that he was too young to be tending to broken parents when he had a broken world to fix.

"Mother?"

By the time Frankie had managed to disentangle himself from his father, the two of them were alone. Or at least, about as alone as you can get on a beach playing host to hundreds of people driven out of their homes by encroaching non-existence.

Frankie stepped into the open doorway of the beach hut. Its front wall tipped away from him, propped up by part of the roof. There wasn't much space inside, certainly not enough space to hide Mother, even though she was small.

"She can't have gone far," said Father.

But she never used to go *anywhere* if she could help it. Not since Grace's accident.

Frankie looked around. There wasn't any sign of her.

He was torn. He wanted to get away, look for Cindy and try to track down this mysterious Owner. And he wanted to know that Mother was safe. But how could he leave Father now?

"If only I had been a child blessed with no imagination," he sighed, and sat heavily on the sand.

Mother came back a short time later.

She had a new, determined look on her face, and dirty, sooty marks on her cheeks and hands.

"Right, now," she said. "There'll be no more talk of going back to work in *that* place, do you hear?"

Frankie looked at her, puzzled.

"What place?" asked Father.

She wiped her grubby hands down her cardigan.

"*That* place," she said, jerking a thumb over her shoulder towards the pier.

Frankie's eyes followed the direction of her gesture.

His brain was struggling to catch up. He almost felt he could hear it whirring and clicking, a mechanical computing machine that couldn't quite keep pace.

Mother.

The pier.

No more... never again.

He looked, and he realised that the smudge of grey staining

the sky just above the pier was smoke and that the smoke must therefore be coming from the pier itself.

Smoke. Pier. Smoke from pier.

"The pier's on fire," he gasped. "Someone's set fire to the pier."

Mother grinned, and wiped at the smut marks on her face with the cuff of her cardigan.

Not just someone.

Mother had set fire to the pier!

"Stay here!" Frankie commanded them. "Just... stay here."

He ran down the beach, kicking dry sand in his wake. Once on the firmer wet sand, he turned and ran as fast as his legs would carry him along the beach towards the pier.

What if Cindy or any of her child followers were trapped in their hiding place beneath the pier? No one would find them. No one would even know to look.

Closer to the pier, he saw that the fire had taken hold of the covered area that housed the dodgems and the amusement arcade. Black smoke billowed upwards, and now Frankie could see livid flames reaching out of the windows and spreading along the walls.

Bells rang out, as the fire brigade arrived. Up on the prom Frankie saw a horse-drawn wagon bearing a huge barrel. Two firemen cranked a hand pump, forcing a feeble jet of water down a hose held by others.

Frankie ran beneath the pier and looked up. He could see patches where the floor timbers had blackened with the heat. "Cindy!" he called. "Wookie!"

He hurried out into the open, and tried to find the gap from which he had emerged that night he had been locked inside the pier. There was no sign of it.

This world was Frankie's. He couldn't see the gaps.

He clenched his fists in sheer frustration.

The ladder! If he could get along the pier, maybe he could get down the ladder and check out the hiding place that way?

He climbed the broken stairway to the prom.

Grace was there.

She stood before him, arms folded across her chest, that old angry look in her flinty eyes.

"No, Fran," she hissed. "You're not going out there. Keep out of it."

"I have to," he told her. "Don't get in my way."

He sidestepped, but she did the same.

The broken-up surface of the prom made evading her difficult, and anyway, she had always been faster than Frankie.

"I have to get through," he pleaded.

She shook her head. "There's nothing for you out there, Frannie. Don't keep interfering. We can still patch things up. We can still be a family again. You just need to believe."

He shook his head. He had things to do.

He ran at a tipped-p block of the promenade, and used its angle to suddenly change direction and keep going.

He heard Grace gasp behind him, then she was at his shoulder, darting past, stopping in front of him.

"No!" she screeched.

As he watched, she crumbled to dust before his eyes. Just as he wondered what was happening, he felt the ground shudder. He thought it was another shift in Faraway's reality, but then he saw clay-coloured hands wrapped around the edges of the slab on which he stood, shaking it, trying to tip it further.

He stumbled back, and the slab flew aside. Mud flowed upwards into the air, limbs and body taking shape, then a head, seaweed hair sprouting.

Grace stood before him again, arms spread as if conducting an orchestra.

He felt the ground shuddering once more, and when he looked down he saw hands gripping the slab he was standing on.

He stepped back, and the slab was hurled aside.

He watched as another mud figure rose from the ground. This one was cruder, barely taking human form and showing no nose, no eyes or mouth, no hair. The thing stepped towards him.

He looked at Grace.

She was smiling unevenly. "Don't come any closer," she told him.

To his right, another slab shifted, and another figure emerged.

To his left, another...

He turned to flee, but the alleyways had all been squeezed shut. He looked around again. Where to go?

"Frankie! Up here!"

He looked up.

A head and shoulders broke the skyline, hanging down from a rooftop several storeys up.

Cindy!

16. The Parting Of The Ways

But how?

When Frankie looked up again, Cindy had gone. Had he imagined her up there, hanging over the gutter, calling down to him?

"This way, Frankie!"

She had appeared again, a little further along. She was gesturing, waving him on.

But... He was surrounded by Grace and her clay army.

He reached down and picked up one of the displaced paving slabs. It was heavier than he'd expected. He struggled to imagine it lighter and then hurled it at the nearest clay figure.

Heavier! The slab was stone: thick, dense rock.

It struck the figure in the chest and knocked it backward.

Frankie ran straight at it. As the figure fell over, clutching the slab to its chest, Frankie jumped.

He landed on the slab and immediately swung forward, leaping clear.

He never had been any good at the triple jump at school. Mr Witsend used to make him do it for a laugh. Watch the fat kid tangle up his feet and end up face-first in the sand pit. If only he could have seen him now!

He kept running until a shout from above stopped him again.

It was Wookie this time. He was on a black metal fire escape, which was all very well except the steps only came down as far as the first floor of the building.

Frankie stood there, staring up.

"Okay," he said. "So what next?"

Wookie grinned and then slid a ladder down from its mounting until it hit the ground right in front of Frankie.

Frankie put a foot on the bottom rung. Why did Cindy always make him so dizzy these days? It was either the first stirrings of lurrrrve or the simple fact that the last couple of times he'd joined up with her he'd ended up on ladders and flimsy platforms having to confront his long-established, and rather intense, distrust of heights.

On reflection, he thought it was probably the latter.

He forced himself up the ladder, until he reached the platform at the foot of the fire escape proper, where he joined Wookie.

"So, Cindy," he said. "You've found another gap."

She nodded.

They sat in a valley between two ridges of rooftop. Cindy and Wookie and Ella were here, and other members of the ragamuffin gang were scattered about over the rooftops. A short distance away, Mr Cray, still in his Jolly Old Sea Captain guise, sat with his back to a chimney, staring into space.

It was like a different world up here. All the buildings had squeezed together so much that their roofs formed a near-continuous landscape of tiles, chimney pots and guttering. A little further along, the spire of a church Frankie couldn't even remember poked crookedly at the sky. All about them, huge gulls wheeled and soared, screeching as they came into land and feed their enormous fluffy chicks.

"I was worried about you all," Frankie said. "When my mother set fire to the pier I came rushing back here to make sure you were okay. That place you were staying under the pier... nobody would have found you there."

Cindy smiled. "Thanks, Frankie. That's sweet. Interesting family you've got. A mum who's handy with the Swan Vestas. A sister who... well, we saw your sister and her earthenware mates. Has your old man got any special gifts, too, just to complete the set?"

Frankie shrugged. "He's just my father," he said. "He thinks he's responsible for everything and he thinks he's failed at everything he's tried. He has trouble seeing all the things he gets right."

Cindy nodded.

He looked around. "So this is your new hiding place," he said. "How many of you are there now?" Kids were scattered about on the rooftops for as far as he could see.

"Don't know," said Cindy. "I stopped counting them after I ran out of fingers. There's a lot of people with no place for them anymore."

Frankie nodded towards Mr Cray. "What about him?" he asked.

"Kind of sad, don't you think?" said Cindy. "This place found him a role as close as it could to the one that was squeezed out of existence. So he goes around scaring children. He isn't very good at it."

"He wasn't very good in his last role, either," chipped in Wookie, who was sitting with them.

"He tried," said Frankie. He'd always had Mr Cray down as B+ for effort, D- for achievement.

"He's okay," said Cindy. "He looks out for us. It was Mr Cray who showed us the way up here in the first place. This is where he used to hide out during daylight. It's like with anything," she continued, "you've got to take the positives from it. I reckon Mr Cray's found what he's best at, for a start. And I never wanted to be stuck in that grubby little shop, either."

"And look at me," chipped in Wookie with a big grin. "I've learnt how to pick pockets. And Ella here has taught me how to burp the alphabet. What more could I want out of life?"

Frankie leaned back onto the slope of a roof. It seemed so peaceful up here, after all that had gone before. Apart from Wookie burping his way through the alphabet, of course, but you could try to blank that out.

All this was an illusion, though, this sense of calm. He knew that this was more like the calm at the eye of the storm. He could smell the burning of the pier, even though the flames had been damped down.

"So how do you get by?" he asked them now.

Cindy shrugged. "We just do," she said. "There's the thieving and the scavenging and all that. Sometimes someone'll buy us chips, you know how it is." She smiled at him when she said that, and that made him think how long ago it seemed, when he and Grace would come down here and share fish and chips with Cindy and the others on the beach.

"It's going to take more than chips, though," she added. "The fog's closing in on us. Pretty soon we won't have anywhere else to run."

He nodded. "I know," he said. "I just needed to work things out."

Cindy hunched forward, elbows on knees, chin on balled fists. "You were looking for me," she said. "I saw your message on the beach before that dog came and rolled in the sand. 'Cindy help - Frankie' – what did you want? What did you think I could do?"

"I was looking for the Owner," explained Frankie.

"But you asked me that before. I already told you: I never met the guy. Just the people he sends to collect the cash."

"But he's hidden away somewhere," said Frankie. "And you're the one person I know who understands how to find the gaps in this place. I thought you might be able to work out where he could be."

She stared at him, and snorted a laugh. "Frankie boy," she said, "you really must have been desperate if that was the best you could come up with! Look at me. I haven't got a clue. It's as much as I can do to keep myself together and keep this lot from falling through the cracks in this place. I don't know why you wanted to come and ask me..."

"So," said Frankie, "how do you do it? How is it that you're able to work this place out better than anyone?"

"I'm not the Owner, if that's what you're thinking!" she laughed. After a pause, she continued: "I just do. Some of us have to live by our wits if we're going to get by. That's how life is... *I* don't know! Anyway: what are you going to do now that I've failed to give you all the answers?"

Frankie smiled. "Come on," he said. He beckoned to her and flipped over onto his hands and knees so he could crawl up the sloping roof.

When he reached the ridge he stopped.

"Don't like heights much, do you?" said Cindy.

Frankie was hanging onto the ridge tiles, his knuckles white. He hooked a crooked arm over, to take his weight. "I always get like this when I'm up on a rooftop four storeys high in a town where buildings sometimes move about for no obvious reason. It's just one of my weaknesses."

"So what did you want to show me?"

From here, they could look down over the ruins of the promenade and the ornamental gardens. Most of the onlookers had gone, but the fire wagon remained, its crew still spraying water over the smouldering remains of the base of the pier.

Grace was still down there, though. She sat alone on a collapsed wall, swinging her feet.

Frankie pointed. "She's on guard," he said.

"Guarding what? And who against?"

"She's guarding the Owner – against me."

Cindy looked at Frankie, waiting for him to explain.

"This place," he said. "It's a place I used to daydream about when we didn't want to hear the rows downstairs. I used to make up stories about Faraway and tell Grace all about it. After she died two years ago... well, everything fell apart. But not here. Not in Faraway. Here it was still possible for the family to be together, for us to be happy. This is the only place she can be alive again."

"And you wanted it badly enough..."

He nodded. "I wanted it badly enough," he agreed. "This is

my world, Cindy. All of it. Mine."

"So... *you're* the Owner?"

He nodded again.

"So... you've found... *yourself*. Game over."

"No," he said. "Here in Faraway there must be another me! The one who sends his representatives out to collect the takings. The one who's still friends with Barking because Grace didn't die here and mess everything up between them." When Grace had run off that day, back in the real world, she had been going to see Barking. She always did after a row with her family. So in Frankie's eyes, Barking was always tied in with Grace's death and the two had ended up bitterest enemies.

"That other me," he continued, "he was the one who tried to warn me off, and told me not to interfere. That wasn't *me* me – that was... the Owner. That was some kind of shadow me, like Grace is a shadow Grace."

"So somewhere out there is another version of you, right? A clay Frankie. What are you and your mud brother going to do, then?"

"I don't know. But I have to find him. Maybe we can work it out together somehow. I think it's the only hope for this place..."

Cindy rolled onto her side to face him, her head resting on a hand. "Okay," she said. "There's you and there's shadow Frankie. All you've got to do now is find him. Back to square one: you don't know where he is!"

But Frankie smiled. "Oh no," he said. "We're way past square one in this game, Cindy. I know exactly where the Owner is. Grace has told me."

17. The Homecoming Queen

She flowed out of a crack in the ground in front of Frankie.

At first it was just a muddy gap between lumps of promenade separated by the upheavals. Then it shifted, bulged, and flowed upwards, taking human form.

Then it was Grace, looking just as she always looked. Frankie's fifteen year-old sister, standing before him, hands on hips, with that determined look of hers.

Frankie faced her. He wasn't going to run this time.

"We can't carry on like this," he told her. "This isn't my dream any more. It's not what I wanted. This isn't the world I used to tell you all about. It's all got out of control."

"This *is* your dream," said Grace. "Or it could be. We had everything, Frannie. We had all that you so desperately wanted. Things were okay again with your world... with *our* world. Why couldn't you have accepted that?"

He stared at her, and felt himself being torn apart. This wasn't Grace before him. And yet... in the sense that she had lived on in people's memories it *was* her.

The tears spilling out of Grace's eyes carved gouges down her muddy cheeks, little river valleys.

"You just need to keep believing!" she demanded.

"I..." But he didn't believe in it. No matter how he tried.

"I'm your *twin*, Frannie! We grew up together, we played together. We did all the things that brothers and sisters are supposed to do. I know all this, Frannie, because it's all up here!" She smacked at the side of her head. "I was there. I remember."

She was very convincing. But she wasn't Grace.

"I... can't," he said. That was all.

He tried to step around her, but she moved across in front of him and they stood, facing each other. "But you *must*, Frannie," she said. "Believe, Frannie. If you want it enough it's true!"

She held her bare arm up towards him.

"Go on," she said. "Touch me. I'm real, Frannie. *Believe*."

Tentatively, he raised his hand. He placed one finger on her forearm and he felt the tiny hairs, the skin. She reached up with her other hand, took his wrist and pressed his hand firmly against her arm. He felt skin that shifted a little across the flesh beneath, and the form of the two bones of the forearm.

He couldn't.

He tightened his grip and jerked his arm down, across, away.

Her arm came away in his hand with a soft tearing sound.

He stared at it in his grip. There was no blood, only soft grey clay at the broken end.

He hurled her arm to the ground and by the time it struck it had hardened, and then it shattered into tiny fragments.

"I'm sorry," he said. "I don't know what you are, but you're not my big sister. I'm sorry." He started to walk.

She bent over and scooped up some of the pieces of her broken arm in her one remaining hand. "Frannie?" she said.

He stopped.

She was scared.

She didn't know what was to come next.

"I'm going to see the Owner," he told her. "We have to sort things out."

"But... but you don't know where he is."

Frankie looked past her to the smoking remains of the pier entrance. "I do," he said. "Why are you so keen to stop me going along the pier? It's the only place I haven't been. He's out there, isn't he, Grace? He's waiting for me to find him. I can feel it."

"But... Frannie, don't be frightened by what you find."

"I know what to expect," he said.

The other him. The shadow Frankie, cast from clay.

The Frankie of this world.

"Then..." Grace shrugged. "I guess I'm not needed any more."

"You'll always be needed, Grace. Look at the mess we all made of things once you'd gone. Me, Mother and Father, Barking."

"But here," she said. She pointed beyond Frankie to where the fog was now curling across the northern end of the prom, around the small harbour. "My time's done, I guess. You cool, Frannie?"

He nodded.

She turned and went to the nearest steps down onto the beach.

Frankie went to stand at a surviving line of railings and watched as she walked across the beach. She was barefoot, and wearing a short, wispy skirt and T-shirt. Her seaweed hair flowed around her, as if picked out by a breeze, even though the air was still.

She came to the water's edge and glanced back over her shoulder.

When a wave reached her, Frankie could see that it washed away part of her lower legs. She stumbled, but kept balance, and stepped deeper into the water.

She dropped to her knees, and leaned back as the gentle waves washed away at her, stripping her down layer by layer, just as the waves would wash away a sandcastle. Hers always were the best.

Soon, all that remained was a big mound of sandy clay, and as Frankie watched even this disappeared and Grace was gone, returned to the sea.

He rubbed at his eyes.

A big wave came in and left a clump of fine, hair-like seaweed on the beach.

Grace!

18. The Owner

Frankie turned to face the pier.

The entrance building, with its swing doors and theatre ticket office still stood, the facade painted in gold and red, but black smudges extended up from the smashed windows and around the door-frames.

Frankie went through the few remaining onlookers and eyed the broken entrance doors.

"You can't go in there, lad," said one of the firefighters. "I think you'll find that anything left standing is going to be closed down for a while."

Frankie went closer and looked inside. There was still a lot of smoke in there, but he could see that the place was in ruins. He doubted he'd be able to get far, even if they would let him through.

He went down to the beach.

Cindy sat on the sand, waiting. "You sure?" she asked, and he nodded. They'd arranged to meet here if he failed the direct approach.

They walked along what had been the base of the promenade. A lot of the blocks still stood here, albeit tipped and jostled at various odd angles.

They came to the upright support posts of the pier. Frankie looked hard at the timbers and the connecting rods and bolts. He looked up at the underside of the pier, and saw dark marks where the fire had reached. He couldn't see how they were going to get through.

Then Cindy put a hand on his arm to get his attention, and pointed.

Between the first upright and the edge of the prom there was a shadow darker than the others, a gap. Cindy stepped through and Frankie followed.

They scrambled up onto a wooden platform. In the gloom, Frankie could see barrels stacked up here, and big shapes covered in tarpaulins.

Cindy had reached into a hiding place somewhere and now had an oil lamp, which she lit, casting a thin light through the chamber.

"This way," she said, gesturing with the lamp.

It was Frankie's turn to put a hand on Cindy's arm. "Thanks," he said. "I'll go on my own. You don't need to come. I'll be okay from here."

"But..."

"You should be looking out for those kids. They're lost without you."

She handed him the lamp. Then she stretched up and kissed him on the cheek. "Take care," she said, and turned, and left.

The air was heavy with the smells of smoke and charred wood. It stung his eyes, and made his throat dry. Coughing only made it worse.

Occasionally, he heard footsteps and shouts from above. Water dripped and streamed down in sudden torrents from the upper level, and it stung Frankie's skin like acid.

He kept going.

He came to a wooden walkway, which was little more than a plank suspended over the sea. He passed along it, and reached an open area, a metal grid balanced between two beams.

Old rags were in heaps and suspended from the beams – hammocks and bed rolls, he realised. This must be where Cindy and her followers had camped out when they were here.

He remembered coming through here with Wookie and Ella, and the shock at suddenly seeing all those faces peering out at him from the shadows.

Eventually, he reached another platform and saw the ladder silhouetted against blue sky.

He climbed up, and swung his legs over the railing at the edge of the pier. Emerging from behind the booth, he looked back. The amusement arcade was in ruins, its roof collapsed. The occasional gaming machine rang a feeble bell, and the weighing machine kept saying, "I speak yuuuuurrrr... I speak yuuuuurrrr..."

Frankie turned.

This was the area where a lot of the new booths and canopies had gone up, but they were all deserted now. No two-headed Lady Euphemia-Eugenie to sup tea with, no waltzing horse or crying, lonely mermaid.

Frankie walked out along the pier, until he was past all this and there was only a wood-floored pier with railings to either side and a line of gas lamps running down the middle.

He squinted.

He couldn't see the end of the pier.

The Owner had hidden himself away out here. It was like a bridge – a bridge to the Faraway version of Frankie.

"Faraway Frankie here I come." He shoved his hands deep in his pockets and walked.

This wasn't going to work. He felt in his guts that this wasn't going to work.

He stopped for a few minutes to gather himself. He sat on one of the many wrought-iron benches that were distributed along the pier.

Looking back, he couldn't see land at all now. At first, the shore had been partly obscured by a layer of haze, but now that had thickened up so that a wall of fog that cut off the view.

It was following him out here.

Ahead, he just saw the pier, extending away to the horizon. He should have borrowed a bicycle, he thought.

He climbed to his feet and set off again.

He had been walking in a straight line for hours, but at any moment he expected to see land, and to find himself walking back into town, just as he had when he had tried to follow the railway and then the beach out of town.

But the alternative... If the fog was following him out here then Frankie and the end of the pier might be all that remained of Faraway now. He thought of his parents, of Cindy, Wookie and the gang, or poor old Mr Cray desperately clinging to existence.

He walked on. He had to see this through.

The end of the pier was ahead of him. He could see it.

He could see the lifeboat station, a single-storey building bulging at the end of the pier, with a launching ramp emerging from the far side.

Some time later Frankie reached the building and went up to the big double doors.

They must have seen him coming. The doors cracked, and one opened outwards. A figure in a baggy grey suit and a tipped back fedora hat emerged, and came to stand in front of Frankie.

Barking. He eyed Frankie, but for a long time said nothing.

"Where is she?" Barking asked, finally, in a voice far softer than normal. "What have you done with her?"

"She's gone," said Frankie. "Grace's time was up."

Barking looked down at the ground. "Thought as much," he said, after a long pause. "Didn't reckon you two could keep it up for long."

Barking jerked his head. "He's inside," he told Frankie. "Good luck."

Frankie went in. It took a moment or two for his eyes to adjust to the change in light levels, then he saw that this building consisted of just a single large room. It was empty, apart from the far end, where a heap of something or other was covered in tarpaulin.

"I told you to keep out of it," said a voice that was horribly familiar. "I instructed people to stop you from messing things up."

Frankie peered into the room, but couldn't make out where his other self was concealed. He stepped across to a wide window and pulled at the cord of a set of blinds.

Light flooded the hall, and Frankie looked, and he saw his other self.

The tarpaulined heap was not some kind of storage area, it was his other self, the shadow Frankie of this world. He was enormous, great mounds of flesh heaped up one layer on top of another.

In the centre, a head nestled down among multiple chins and rolls of neck.

This shadow Frankie stared across at him. "And...?" he demanded. "Have you finished looking?"

Frankie walked closer.

"So what have you come for, then?"

Frankie spread his hands. "I... we've got to sort all this out," he said. "This place... it's falling apart."

A slight movement of Shadow Frankie's head sent a quiver through its supporting chins. "There's nothing to sort out," he said. "I'm comfortable here. This is *my* world. I don't need to sort anything out."

Frankie pointed towards the window. "Look out there," he demanded. Fog was wrapping itself around the building now. "It's all fading away. We're not managing to hold it together."

He saw a worried expression flicker across Shadow Frankie's – *his* – features. He clearly hadn't realised how bad things had become.

"Grace has gone," said Frankie. "You couldn't pull that one off, either."

"That was *your* fault!" snarled Shadow Frankie. "You didn't believe in her. Not even at the beginning."

"You didn't do a good enough job," said Frankie softly. "You never convinced me, no matter how much I tried."

But he hadn't come here to argue with himself... "So what next?" he asked. "What can we do to fix all this?"

Shadow Frankie was watching him, and Frankie couldn't quite work out the expression on his face.

"Game's nearly over," Shadow Frankie gasped. "You've nearly done it."

"Done what?"

"Dug deep," said Shadow Frankie. "Found the real you... the one you were hiding away. The one you were protecting."

"What do you mean? I never *lost* the real me..."

"Look at yourself, Frankie. Go on: look at yourself."

Slowly, Frankie went across to the window. There was a faint reflection of himself against the grey backdrop.

He put a hand up to his face, and felt the channels where the water from the fire hoses had dropped down on him, washing muddy grooves across his features.

He took his hand away and stared at its smooth grey surface.

He turned.

Another quiver of the head.

"Yes," said Shadow Frankie. "I'm the real Frankie, hiding away from the world. And you... you're Faraway Frankie, a part of this world just as Grace is. You're the me I'd like to be, the me I would be if I dared."

Faraway Frankie stared at his shadow self, his *real* self.

He swallowed. Then he shook his head, as if it would shake some sense into it.

"Then *dare*," he said.

"We have to get him out of here," Faraway Frankie told Barking, as the two of them found real Frankie's arms and hauled on them.

"But..." said Barking.

"He's right," said real Frankie. "I want to move. I want to return to the world."

Faraway Frankie tugged and tugged at real Frankie's arm, but it was no good – like trying to pull spaghetti from a plate: one bit moved but the rest just stayed put.

He gestured at Barking and the two of them went behind real Frankie. Burying their shoulders into his flesh, they pushed and, slowly, Frankie started to shift, and then... he had tumbled onto his side, and then his front.

With his hands on the floor, real Frankie pushed, and Faraway Frankie and Barking found handholds and pulled, and then he was up on his feet, swaying, tipping back as if he was about to fall as the two darted clear.

He teetered and swayed. He wobbled. He stayed upright, his face bright pink from the effort.

He beamed at the two. "Right," he said, "what next?"

Faraway Frankie glanced across, and was suddenly grateful to whoever had possessed the foresight to build double doors into this building.

They made it. Progress was slow, but eventually real Frankie was standing in the double doorway, looking out at the blanket of fog that had descended on the pier.

Faraway Frankie looked in the same direction, too. He twitched from foot to foot, and walked around in little circles, unable to hide his impatience.

"You'd better go," said his other self. "Barking and I can manage from here. You go."

Faraway Frankie looked at real Frankie. The big guy meant it. He was going to leave this place, but it would have to be at his own pace.

He looked at Barking, who nodded. "I'll stick with him," he said. "I'll make sure he gets us out of here."

Faraway Frankie hesitated, but his other self nodded.

"Barking's okay, really," he said. "Losing Grace... it hurt him just as it hurt the rest of us. He's okay now, though. We'll be okay."

Faraway Frankie gripped Barking's arm, and then reached across and did the same to his other self. "Thanks," he said, and then he turned and set off.

Fog was all around Faraway Frankie. He moved in the centre of a small clear patch, which at times was so small that he couldn't see the railings to either side. The direction of the planks kept him on course.

He walked fast, and at times he even broke into a run.

He held real Frankie's words in his head.

You... you're Faraway Frankie, a part of this world just as Grace is.

Real Frankie had said *is*, not *was*.

Faraway Frankie smelt burnt wood.

A shape loomed to his left. The booth selling rock and candy floss. The ladder was back there.

He hesitated, then headed on through the burnt ruins of the arcade. The firemen had stopped him entering the pier, but they were hardly going to stop him leaving.

"Hey!" Someone was inside one of the ruined shelters, but Frankie ignored the call and kept walking.

He came to the entrance area. There was no glass in the swing doors, so he stepped right through one door frame, and then through the next.

Out on the broken up promenade he moved across to the steps down to the beach.

How long since he'd last been here?

Time didn't really seem to mean much to him anymore. What mattered was what was in his heart, what he believed.

When his feet hit the sand he started to run. Across, through the loose, dry sand and stones, and over the line of seaweed and flotsam that marked the level of the last high tide.

He stopped before the water.

Are you out there, Grace?

He stepped into the waves. He felt them eating away at his ankles like acid, but then it was more of a gentle fizzing than a burning, and then he realised that he was slumping down into the water, as it soaked away his clay constitution.

Moving on the stumps of his legs now, dissolved up as far as the knees, he stepped forward, deeper into the sea, until the waves lapped at his waist, his chest.

All dissolving away.

Grace!

A ripple in the water. More than just a wave. He was sure it was more than just a wave.

Frankie?

He toppled forward, no longer able to support himself as the water gently tugged him apart.

Epilogue: The Boy Who Found Himself

Frankie Finnegan stood in the doorway and watched the crude clay replica of himself stride away along the pier. Within seconds, the figure was lost in the fog.

"So how're we going to do this then?" asked Barking, eyeing him uncertainly. "You haven't been out of here for ages."

"Piggyback?" suggested Frankie.

He walked instead. It was tough, but something in him had woken up and he was determined to do this. He heaved one leg past the other, allowed his balance to shift, and then swung the other leg. He stopped to rest regularly, and all the time, Barking hovered at his side as if he was ready to catch Frankie if he fell, which would have been quite a sight in itself.

They walked in a clear patch in the fog, a patch that started to expand.

Frankie grew hot very quickly, and he knew he stank of sweat, but Barking didn't say anything. At one point, he realised that the heat wasn't all the result of his exertions. He paused and looked up, and there was a brighter patch of grey in the sky where the sun was starting to break through. Looking back, he couldn't see the end of the pier any more.

As the fog started to thin, the walking came easier to Frankie. He didn't have to think about the swing of each leg, and he wasn't aware of the rasping pain in his chest as he breathed.

Eventually, he even started to feel good, to enjoy the movement, the sense of strength and freedom. He had left something behind out there, and it was more than just the kilos falling away as he walked.

"Come on, Barking," he said, slapping his companion on the

back.

He set off at a jog, then started to run, to sprint, and with every stride he felt himself shedding a burden he had carried for so long.

He stopped, breathing raggedly, leaning against the railings. Barking caught him a few seconds later.

Frankie looked down at the gently surging sea.

"Look!" gasped Barking, pointing.

Frankie did. The promenade stretched out along the edge of the bay, with the houses of Nereby-on-Sea beyond.

They walked on, the air cool, the sky clear.

They came to the amusement arcade and the Deep Sea Aquarium, but everything was boarded up for the winter. They stepped out through the swing doors onto the promenade. The place was quiet, save for an elderly couple walking a terrier, and a juggler somehow managing to keep six balls in the air at a time.

"I'll miss Grace," said Barking softly.

Frankie nodded. "We all will," he said. "We all will."

Then he slapped Barking on the back. "Come on," he said, "I'll race you!".

Life was as sweet as it could be. You couldn't really ask for much more than that, could you?

Frankie lived with his mother in their small terraced house next door to the Jolly Old Sea Captain, and they would do the shopping together, and sometimes just go out and walk along the prom. His father kept trying to do the right thing; he lived in his grubby little bedsit and he visited as often as he could without provoking an argument. Mr Cray tried his best, but still wasn't a particularly good teacher. Wookie remained unrealistically proud of his ability to burp the alphabet, and he and Ella Cochrane had become inseparable.

Cindy still worked up at the cornershop, saving her money so that one day she could quit and go off and find herself, as she put it.

But until she could, she would slip away with Frankie sometimes and the two of them would go down to the promenade, to the stretch just above the pier, where metal steps dropped down to the beach. They would stop here, and look out over the bay, often sitting in silence for hours on end. This suited them both well, for the two of them were dreamers, and neither had a need for many words.

And sometimes one of them would twitch, put a hand on the other's arm, and point, imagining that they had glimpsed the boy and his sister who were now a part of the sea.

THE END

The Bitten Word

A collection of all-new vampire stories, with front cover art by John Kaiine and back cover art by award-winning artist Les Edwards.

Available in two editions: A5 paperback   £9.99
And a Special Signed Hardback edition, with dust jacket, limited to just 150 copies; with each copy individually numbered and signed by all the authors.   £32.00

 The limited edition hardback includes a bonus story by award-winning author Ian Watson, plus a colour plate of Les Edwards' wonderful back cover picture, *Descending*.

Full contents:
1. **Ian Whates** – Introduction
2. **Simon Clark** – Vampithecus
3. **Kelley Armstrong** – Young Bloods
4. **Sarah Singleton** – A Winter's Tale
5. **Gary McMahon** – Those Damned Kids
6. **Storm Constantine** – Where the Vampires Live
7. **John Kaiine** – English Spoken
8. **Chaz Brenchley** – Hothouse Flowers
9. **Nancy Kilpatrick** – Traditions in Future Perfect
10. **Andrew Hook** – Red or White
11. **Freda Warrington** – Fall of the House of Blackwater
12. **Tanith Lee** – Taken at His Word
13. **Kari Sperring** – Cold Rush
14. **Donna Scott** – Lord of the Lyceum
15. **Sam Stone** – Fool's Gold
16. **Jon Courtenay Grimwood** – Wuthering Bites
17. **Ian Whates** – The Abomination of Beauty
18. **Gail Z Martin** – Vanities
19. **Ian Watson** – My Vampire Cake* (*Available only in the Special Signed Limited Edition)

New From Newcon Press: www.newconpress.co.uk

CONFLICTS

– A spaceship hurtles into the unknown carrying humanity's last hope, but does it also carry the seeds of its own doom? –

– The galaxy's ultimate facilitator finds himself pursued by relentless enemies, while, of greater importance, there's a puzzle to be solved –

– A rescue mission to a hostile alien world turns out to be far more than it seems –

Thirteen tales of human striving, of ingenuity, brilliance, desperate action, violence, and resolution. Thirteen tales of Conflict, of Science Fiction at its absolute best.

Contents: